COUNTRIES OF THE WORLD

Venezuela

Gareth Stevens Publishing
A WORLD ALMANAC EDUCATION GROUP COMPANY

About the Author: Dr. William Wardrope is part of the Latin American business faculty at Southwest Texas State University. Dr. Wardrope has published work in several academic journals and is also a freelance writer. The recipient of many teaching and research awards, he travels extensively to Latin America and visited Venezuela in spring of 2002.

Written by
WILLIAM WARDROPE

Edited by
SELINA KUO

Edited in the U.S. by
GUS GEDATUS
ALAN WACHTEL

Designed by
BENSON TAN

Picture research by
SUSAN JANE MANUEL

First published in North America in 2003 by
Gareth Stevens Publishing
A World Almanac Education Group Company
330 West Olive Street, Suite 100
Milwaukee, Wisconsin 53212 USA

Please visit our web site at:
www.garethstevens.com
For a free color catalog describing
Gareth Stevens Publishing's list of high-quality
books and multimedia programs, call
1-800-542-2595 (USA) or 1-800-387-3178 (Canada).
Gareth Stevens Publishing's fax: (414) 332-3567.

© **TIMES MEDIA PRIVATE LIMITED 2003**
Originated and designed by
Times Editions
An imprint of Times Media Private Limited
A member of the Times Publishing Group
Times Centre, 1 New Industrial Road
Singapore 536196
http://www.timesone.com.sg/te

Library of Congress Cataloging-in-Publication Data
Wardrope, William.
Venezuela / by William Wardrope.
p. cm. — (Countries of the world)
Includes bibliographical references and index.
Summary: An overview of Venezuela that includes information on its geography, history, government, language, culture, and current issues.
ISBN 0-8368-2369-9 (lib. bdg.)
1. Venezuela—Juvenile literature. [1. Venezuela.] I. Title.
II. Countries of the world (Milwaukee, Wis.)
F2308.5.W37   2003
987—dc21   2003042737

Printed in Singapore

1 2 3 4 5 6 7 8 9 06 05 04 03

Contents

AN OVERVIEW OF VENEZUELA

The República Bolivariana de Venezuela, or the Bolivarian Republic of Venezuela, is one of twelve South American countries. Before gaining independence in 1829, Venezuela was a Spanish colony for three centuries. Today, the country is one of the more modernized South American nations and benefits from its wealth of natural resources. Venezuela's indigenous peoples, however, face an uncertain future because twentieth-century industrialization has destroyed many of their natural living environments. Throughout history, Venezuelans have proved to be a fiercely resilient people, and their culture continues to reflect their strength with which they have always led their lives.

Opposite: **Venezuelans in the district of El Rosal, in Caracas, use a crosswalk on a rainy day. The city of Caracas has a population of over 3 million people.**

Below: **Many children in the Orinoco Delta region live with few basic necessities. Most of the Orinoco Delta lies in Delta Amacuro, one of the country's poorest states.**

THE FLAG OF VENEZUELA

First adopted in 1930, the current Venezuelan flag consists of (from top to bottom) equally sized, horizontal bands of yellow, blue, and red. The country's coat of arms is positioned near the left edge of the yellow band, and seven white, five-pointed stars rise and fall in a semicircular curve at the center of the blue band. The stars represent the seven settlements that first united against Spanish rule under the 1811 Independence Act. These settlements were Caracas, Cumaná, Barcelona, Barinas, Margarita, Mérida, and Trujillo. In Venezuela, flags raised for civilian purposes do not usually bear the coat of arms.

Geography

Venezuela covers a total area of 352,051 square miles (912,050 square kilometers) and is the sixth-largest country in South America. The country is bordered by the Caribbean Sea to the north, the Atlantic Ocean to the northeast, Guyana to the east, Brazil to the south and southeast, and Colombia to the west. The Venezuelan coastline measures about 1,740 miles (2,800 kilometers) long, and seventy-two nearby islands are also part of Venezuelan territory.

Mainland Venezuela can be divided into three main geographical regions: the Cordillera, the Llanos, and the Guiana Highlands. The Cordillera is the mountainous region in northwestern Venezuela. The Andes mountain chain, which extends north from Colombia into Venezuela, begins to fork just south of the city of Colón. The western range, the Sierra de Perijá, roughly outlines Venezuela's western border, while the eastern

MARGARITA ISLAND

Isla de Margarita, or Margarita Island, is located about twenty-three miles (37 km) off the eastern section of the Venezuelan coastline. The island is a favorite holiday destination for many Venezuelans.
(A Closer Look, page 58)

COASTAL CORDILLERA

The coastal Cordillera, or Cordillera de la Costa, is a series of mountains that stretches for 447 miles (720 km) along the Venezuelan coastline, from the state of Yaracuy to the very tip of the Paria Peninsula. Venezuela's coastal mountains occupy only 3 percent of the country's area, but the stretch of undulating terrain is home to the highest concentration of Venezuelans. Major cities, such as Caracas, Valencia, and Maracay, are located in the valleys of these coastal mountains.

Left: A woman makes her way through parts of the Venezuelan Andes in the state of Mérida.

Left: The Orinoco River has an odd branch that flows inland to join the Casiquiare River, which is shown here. The Casiquiare River mainly drains the southernmost state of Amazonas, where tropical rain forests dominate the terrain.

LAKE MARACAIBO

Lago de Maracaibo, or Lake Maracaibo, is famous as South America's largest lake. Located between the Sierra de Perijá and the Sierra de Mérida, the lake measures about 100 miles (161 km) from north to south and seventy-five miles (121 km) from east to west at its widest point.

(A Closer Look, page 56)

ANGEL FALLS

Located in the eastern Guiana Highlands, Churún-Merú is the world's highest waterfall, with a drop of 3,212 feet (979 m). Churún-Merú is also known as Salto Angel, or Angel Falls.

THE CAPITAL CITY OF CARACAS

Nicknamed the "City of Eternal Spring," Caracas was founded in 1567 and remains the country's political, economic, and cultural hub.

(A Closer Look, page 48)

range, the Sierra de Mérida, extends northeast toward the city of Barquisimeto. Part of the Sierra de Mérida, Pico Bolívar, or Bolívar Peak, is the country's highest peak, at 16,428 feet (5,007 meters).

The Llanos, or the Plains, is an enormous area of low, flat grassland in central Venezuela. Situated between the Sierra de Mérida and the Rio Orinoco, the Llanos extend for about 800 miles (1,287 km) from east to west and cover about one-third of Venezuela's area.

The Guiana Highlands occupies nearly half of mainland Venezuela and dominates the country's south and southeast. Also the country's most remote region, the Guiana Highlands is a vast upland area covered with lush, tropical vegetation and dotted with massive granite formations that have been described as "table mountains." Table mountains differ from typical mountains in that they have flat tops and straight, vertical sides.

Rio Orinoco

Rio Orinoco, or the Orinoco River, is Venezuela's primary natural drainage channel. The river flows for a total of 1,590 miles (2,560 km) from its source in the Sierra Parima, or the Parima Mountains, in the southern Guiana Highlands, to the Atlantic Ocean via a long, meandering path through the Llanos. The Caroní River is the Orinoco River's main tributary.

A Tropical Climate

Venezuela has a national average annual temperature of 82° Fahrenheit (28° Celsius), and over 90 percent of the country has an average annual temperature of 75° F (24° C) or warmer. Because Venezuela is in the tropics, altitude is the only cause of variations in regional temperatures. Many regions have average annual temperatures that differ insignificantly — by only 1.8° F (1° C) to 9° F (5° C). The average annual temperatures of some regions, such as the cities of Mérida and Maracaibo, may appear to differ substantially. Considering the altitudinal difference of nearly 5,000 feet (1,524 m) between the two cities, however, makes the 16.2° F (9° C) difference in temperature remarkably mild and relatively negligible. In Venezuela, only regions above 6,562 feet (2,000 m) have temperatures under 75° F (24° C). Regions above 9,843 feet (3,000 m) have average temperatures under 46° F (8° C) and tend to be covered with snow.

Left: Venezuela's position near the equator gives the country a tropical climate that undergoes few changes in a year. Venezuelan vegetation is mostly tropical or subtropical and is usually evergreen. Forests cover between 30 and 40 percent of the country, while savanna grasses, or tall, coarse grasses that tend to flourish in plains, cover up to 50 percent of Venezuela's land.

Plants and Animals

The country's vegetation, much like its climate, also varies with altitude. Below 1,500 feet (457 m), Venezuela's plant life is mostly tropical. In the country's subtropical zones, above 1,500 feet (457 m), plants typically include tree ferns and orchids. Above 5,000 feet (1,524 m), subtropical vegetation thins into mountain vegetation, and above 10,000 feet (3,048 m), only a few species of small, alpine shrubs and lichens survive. Lichens usually appear as crusty patches on tree trunks or rocks.

Venezuela is remarkably rich in animal life, although most species found in the country are also common to the rest of northern South America. The Venezuelan forests are home to several species of monkeys, bears, deer, and cats such as jaguars and pumas. A generous variety of snakes also resides in Venezuelan forests. Venomous snakes include coral snakes and striped rattlesnakes, while nonvenomous snakes include the mighty boa constrictor and the enormous anaconda. Venezuela's bird life is also especially impressive. More than 1,300 species of birds have been spotted in the country. The figure is equivalent to about 42 percent of all birds known to South America and about 14 percent known to the world.

PINK DOLPHINS

The world's largest freshwater dolphin, the pink dolphin is also known by a host of other names, including the Amazon dolphin, boto vermelho, bouto, inia, and the pink porpoise.

(A Closer Look, page 62)

History

Native Peoples

The earliest known inhabitants of Venezuela were Stone Age people believed to have descended from the prehistoric people who, near the end of the Ice Age, migrated from Asia to North America via a land bridge over the Bering Sea. Migrating farther south, they reached what is now western Venezuela about 10,000 B.C. and practiced food gathering and hunting using simple tools made from stones, bones, and wood.

Venezuela's first Indians were gradually replaced by more evolved groups, which mainly consisted of Arawaks, Caribs, and Chibchas. In the course of several thousand years, the Arawaks, who were a relatively peaceful people, came to occupy Venezuela's coastal regions in large communities. The Caribs, who were fiercely aggressive and cannibalistic, mostly settled on the islands off the Venezuelan coast, such as those between

AMERINDIANS IN VENEZUELA

Amerindians, or American Indians, are the various tribes of native Indians in the Americas as a whole. Today, only about 2 percent of Venezuelans are Amerindian. The Warao and Yanomami tribes form two of the larger surviving Amerindian cultures. The effects of industrialization have forced many members of these tribes to abandon their traditional ways of life and adopt more modern and westernized lifestyles (*above*).

(*A Closer Look, page 44*)

Left: This illustration is an artist's impression of a native Indian roaming the lush, tropical rain forest in the Americas.

Left: In 1498, Italian explorer Christopher Columbus became the first known European to reach the land that is today Venezuela. Columbus, who was employed by the Spanish at that time, claimed his discovery for Spain. Cumaná, Venezuela's first permanent Spanish settlement, was not established until 1523.

and including modern-day Puerto Rico and Trinidad and Tobago. The Chibchas in Venezuela tended to settle in the valleys of the Andes and were the most advanced of the country's various native Indian tribes. Apart from these three main tribes that formed permanent settlements, numerous smaller, nomadic groups roamed the Llanos and the areas around Lake Maracaibo.

The Early Europeans

The Spanish knew of Venezuela as early as 1498 but were, at first, unenthusiastic about colonizing the area. Merchants from rival European countries, such as England and France, were allowed to freely exploit Venezuelan resources provided they had trading licenses purchased from the Spanish government. The Europeans who visited Venezuela during this time were mainly motivated by the lucrative promise of pearl fishing, and they tended not to venture beyond the country's northeastern coastal regions.

European attention soon turned to northwestern Venezuela, where gold mining was already commonplace for the local Chibchas. In 1528, Welser, a family-owned, German bank, bought from the Spanish government the rights to exploit and colonize the area. Wesler's venture, however, proved to be unprofitable, and by 1546, the area again came under Spanish rule. It was not until the second half of the sixteenth century that the Spanish intensifed their efforts to colonize Venezuela.

Spanish Colonization

By 1600, more than twenty Spanish settlements had been established in Venezuela, including Caracas, founded in 1567. The settlements were located either in the valleys of the Andes or along the Caribbean coast. Many native Indians were enslaved and forced to dive for pearls, mine for gold, or cultivate valuable crops, such as sugar, tobacco, and cacao, for Spanish gains. The Indians resented colonial rule, but their rebellions were always crushed. Bloody clashes with the Spanish, however, did not claim as many lives as the diseases, such as malaria, smallpox, and typhus, that were introduced to Venezuela by the Europeans. Following the deaths of masses of Indian slaves from these diseases, the Spanish brought many African slaves to Venezuela to alleviate the labor shortage. Despite Spanish efforts, the colony's economy enriched mainly the English and the French in the 1500s and the Dutch in the 1600s. By 1728, a group of Spanish merchants established *Real Compañía Guipuzcoana de Caracas*, a trading company that sought to monopolize trade between Venezuela and Spain. With support from the Spanish government, the merchants succeeded in 1732. The company's profits soared in the 1730s and 1740s, partly because of sharp increases in demand from Europe and the American colonies for cacao. The company's policies,

ETHNICITY AND CLASS IN COLONIAL VENEZUELA

Apart from the Spaniards who occupied top government and church positions, the colonial upper class consisted of Creoles, or Venezuelan-born whites. Most Creoles were landowners and, thus, controlled much of the colony's trade and wealth. Mestizos were people of mixed white and African or Amerindian descent. Although the mestizos generally did not own property and had no social status or political influence, they were still better off than the colony's enslaved, population, which consisted of native Indians and Africans.

Left: Founded in 1611, Jajo is a tiny town in the mountains of the state of Trujillo. The town's original colonial architecture and narrow, winding roads have been carefully preserved.

however, grew increasingly unreasonable and disadvantaged Venezuelan growers. In the mid-1700s, rioting Venezuelans put enough pressure on the government in Spain to reduce the company's privileges. The company dissolved in the 1780s.

The Long Road to Independence

A group of Creoles first called for Venezuela's independence in 1797, but they were quickly silenced by the government in Caracas. By 1810, the Creoles overthrew Venezuela's top Spanish officials, and under the guidance of Simón Bolívar, a dedicated freedom fighter, and General Francisco de Miranda, a career soldier, Venezuela's independence was declared on July 5, 1811.

Spain soon counterattacked, and Venezuela was reabsorbed. Bolívar, in the meantime, escaped to New Granada (present-day Colombia and Panama), where he gathered enough support to launch another attempt at liberating Venezuela. In 1813, Bolívar's forces won Venezuela but lost it again in 1814.

In 1815, Spain sent a large army under General Pablo Morillo to reestablish colonial power in New Granada and Venezuela. After fighting for two years in New Granada, Morillo and his men entered Venezuela and killed countless resisting Venezuelans. Spanish power waned decisively only after Bolívar's forces won a landmark victory at Carabobo in 1821. Newly freed Venezuela soon became part of Gran Colombia, a short-lived republic that had been set up by Bolivar in 1819.

SIMÓN BOLÍVAR: FOUNDING FATHER

In the early nineteenth century, Simón Bolívar, the freedom fighter who became Venezuela's national hero, tirelessly led the independence movement that ultimately freed a significant portion of South America.

(*A Closer Look*, page 68)

THE REPUBLIC OF GRAN COLOMBIA

In 1819, Bolívar freed Bogotá, New Granada's capital, and the Republic of Gran Colombia, a union of Venezuela, New Granada, and Quito (present-day Ecuador), was formed. The Spanish repeatedly tried to quash the new republic but were unsuccessful. Venezuela broke free from Gran Colombia in 1829.

Left: **In 1998, Hugo Rafael Chavez Frías, a former paratrooper, won Venezuela's presidential election in a landslide victory.**

From Caudillismo to Democracy

From 1830 to 1935, Venezuela endured one military dictatorship after another. The period came to be known as "Caudillismo." Caudillos, or provincial military leaders, were allied with the country's Conservative and Liberal parties and engaged in fierce power struggles, which led to a bloody civil war (1859–1863) and two constitutional changes (1864 and 1872).

Venezuelan presidents following the last caudillo restored civil liberties and improved public services such as health care and education. In 1945, Democratic Action, a political party supported by a majority of Venezuelans, rose to power. The country's first taste of democracy, however, ended in 1948, when the conservatives led a successful military coup. By 1951, harsh authoritarian rule had returned to Venezuela under President Marcos Pérez Jiménez, who was eventually overthrown in 1958.

Venezuela prospered in the 1970s, during which the selling price of oil increased fourfold. By the late 1970s, however, worldwide economic recessions and increasing domestic poverty brewed renewed political unrest and civil strife. In 1989, President Carlos Andrés Pérez Rodriguez introduced a series of belt-tightening economic policies that sparked a bloody riot that left hundreds dead. By the mid-1990s, two bloody military coups had been mounted, and Pérez was removed on charges of corruption.

THE LAST CAUDILLO

In 1908, General Juan Vicente Gómez came to power. Under his leadership, Venezuela's economy strengthened considerably because of a sharp increase in foreign investments aimed at developing the country's oil industry. Investors, however, were only forthcoming because of the country's stability, which Gómez forcibly achieved by ruling Venezuela as a police state.

POLITICAL UNREST IN 2002

President Hugo Chavez, who had earlier been imprisoned for his role in a coup against President Carlos Andrés Pérez Rodriguez, was himself the target of a military coup in April 2002. Chavez was removed from office and held in military custody but returned to power two days later.
(*A Closer Look, page 64*)

José Antonio Páez (1790–1873)

A forerunner of the Caudillismo era, General José Antonio Páez led Venezuela's declaration of independence in 1830 and undertook the difficult task of stabilizing a country ravaged by years of fighting and chaos. Although he ruled with an iron fist, Páez had provided Venezuelans with eighteen years of peace and economic progress by the time he was overthrown and exiled in 1848. A staunch conservative, Páez served as president for two nonconsecutive, four-year terms beginning in 1831 and 1839. In the years before and after his second term, Páez continued to control Venezuela via the puppet leaders who replaced him. Páez spent his last few years in New York City, where he wrote his autobiography.

José Antonio Páez

Rómulo Gallegos Freire (1884–1969)

A prolific writer, Rómulo Gallegos wrote extensively and insightfully about Venezuelan life and politics before he became president in December 1947. He was the first president approved by a majority of the Venezuelan people. Under Gallegos, Venezuelans received generous government funding in health care, housing, and education, as well as agricultural and industrial development. As a literary figure, Gallegos is best remembered for his first novel, *Doña Bárbara* (1929), which was translated into English in 1931. His other works include *Pobre negro* (1937), or *Poor Black*, and *La rebelión y otros cuentos* (1947), or *The Rebellion and Other Stories*.

Rómulo Gallegos Freire

Irene Sáez Conde (1961–)

Irene Sáez Conde first became famous in 1981, when she won the Miss Universe beauty pagent. In 1989, she graduated from Universidad Central de Venezuela, or the Central University of Venezuela, with a degree in political science. From 1992 to 1998, Sáez Conde was the mayor of the municipality of Chacao in Caracas. In addition to improving public services, including education, health care, security, and sanitation, Sáez Conde also sought to provide Chacao residents with various social development and community-building programs. In 1998, Sáez Conde ran for president but was unsuccessful. From 1999 to 2000, she served as the governor of the state of Nueva Esparta.

Government and the Economy

A Federal Republic

Venezuela is officially identified as a federal republic, which means that the country's constitution draws on a mixture of republican, democratic, and federalist principles.

The Venezuelan government consists of three branches: executive, legislative, and judicial. The executive branch is led by the president, who, after the 1999 revision of the constitution, is also the head of government and the Venezuelan armed forces. The president is popularly elected to serve a six-year term and is assisted by a cabinet of ministers, called the Council of Ministers, all of whom are appointed by the president. Under the revised constitution, the president is entitled to immediate reelection, an unprecedented move in Venezuelan democratic history.

The legislative branch consists of a unicameral, or one-house, congress. Called Asamblea Nacional, or National Assembly, the Venezuelan congress is made up of 165 members, who are elected by the Venezuelan people to serve five-year terms. Following the 1999 revision of the constitution, three of the 165 seats must be filled by persons of indigenous descent.

Opposite: The local government office for the state of Zulia is located in the city of Maracaibo.

CONSTITUTIONAL RIGHTS

The Venezuelan constitution guarantees freedom of expression, freedom of religion, and equal rights for men and women. All Venezuelans aged eighteen and above are eligible to vote.

Left: Venezuelan parliamentary sessions are held in the Capitolio Nacional, or National Capitol.

Venezuela's judicial branch is headed by the Tribuna Suprema de Justica, or the Supreme Tribunal of Justice. The highest court in the country, the tribunal oversees a system of lower courts that include civil, criminal, constitutional, and political-administrative. Members of the tribunal are elected by the Asamblea Nacional for single, non-renewable twelve-year terms.

Local Government

Venezuela is divided into twenty-five administrative regions. The country contains twenty-three states, or *estados* (ehs-TAH-dohs); the federal district, or *distrito federal* (dees-TREE-toh feh-deh-RAHL); and the federal dependency, or *dependencia federal* (deh-penn-DEHN-see-ah feh-deh-RAHL). The federal district is also known as the capital district, and it includes the city of Caracas. The federal dependency is made up of eleven island groups that are made up of a total of seventy-two Caribbean islands.

An elected governor leads each administrative region. Each region is divided into districts, and each district is run by an elected mayor. Both governors and mayors are elected to four-year terms and are allowed to be relected once.

THE MILITARY

The Venezuelan military is organized in a unified front, called the Fuerzas Armadas Nacionales (FAN), or the National Armed Forces. FAN consists of four branches: Fuerzas Ejercito (Ground Forces), Fuerzas Armada (Naval Forces), Fuerzas Aviacion (Air Force), and Guardia Nacional (National Guard).

Male Venezuelans become eligible for military service at the age of eighteen. In 2001, more than 6.5 million Venezuelans were available for military service but only 4.7 million were considered fit. Men aged fifty and older do not perform military service.

The Economy

In 2002, the Venezuelan economy crashed because of President Hugo Chavez's radical economic reform policies. Chavez aimed to reduce the country's overreliance on oil and to reduce the vast and widening gap between the country's rich and poor. Although his ideas seemed sensible, his methods were questionable. Petróleos de Venezuela, S. A. (PDVSA), Venezuela's state-owned oil monopoly, suffered greatly under the Chavez government. PDVSA was subjected to ultrahigh taxes, increased bureaucratic interference, and the removal of nineteen senior executives. As a result, PDVSA, which had been achieving double-digit growth for many consecutive years up until 2000, reported a drastic drop in earnings for 2001 and a further decrease for 2002.

In 2000, Venezuela had a workforce that was fast approaching 10 million people and an unemployment rate of about 14 percent. According to Venezuela's Central Bank, the rate of inflation rose from 12.3 percent in 2001 to 31.2 percent in 2002. More than half of Venezuelans were already living below the poverty line before the 2002 economic crisis.

BLESSED WITH "BLACK GOLD"

In 1922, George Reynolds discovered Venezuela's first major oil field, La Rosa, in the state of Zulia. Reynolds was a manager with Shell at the time. By 1928, Venezuela was the world's second-largest exporter of oil, after the United States.

(A Closer Look, page 46)

SAVING VENEZUELA: ENVIRONMENTAL PROJECTS

Venezuela's rapid industrialization in the 1900s endangered natural treasures such as the Amazonian rain forests and the Caribbean ecosystem. A number of large corporations and nonprofit organizations (NGOs) have since joined hands in an effort to reduce damage to Veneuzela's environment.

(A Closer Look, page 66)

Left: The Venezuelan oil industry has more or less single-handedly supported the country's economy since the 1920s. Despite efforts to diversify Venezuela's economy in the 1990s, non-petroleum products still accounted for only about 20 percent of the country's total exports. Before 2002, the oil industry consistently contributed about one-third of the country's gross domestic product.

Agriculture

Agriculture employs about 13 percent of the Venezuelan workforce and provides about 5 percent of the country's gross domestic product (GDP). Venezuelan farmers grow a wide variety of food crops, including coffee, corn, rice, sorghum, bananas, and sugarcane. The Llanos provides extensive cattle grazing land, while the country's coastal regions are rich with fish and shellfish.

Industry

Venezuela has three main types of industries: oil refining and petrochemical producing, mining and metal processing, and consumer goods manufacturing. Oil refineries and petrochemical plants are concentrated in or near the cities of Morón and Puerto Cabello and in the state of Zulia. Manufacturers of consumer goods, on the other hand, are found in the country's larger cities, such as Valencia, Maracay, Caracas, and Barquisimeto. Venezuela's manufacturing sector produces textiles, leather, paper, and home appliances, such as washing machines, television sets, and radios. Heavy industries, which include mining operations and metalworks producing iron, steel, and aluminum, are mostly situated in Ciudad Guayana.

MAJOR TRADE PARTNERS AND EXPORTS

In the late 1990s, the United States was the single largest buyer of Venezuelan exports. In 1998 and 1999, the United States purchased over 50 percent of all Venezuelan exports. Venezuela's other trading partners include Brazil, Colombia, Japan, Italy, France, Germany, and Canada.

Petroleum and its by-products, or petrochemicals, steel, aluminum (*below*), bauxite, agricultural produce, and consumer goods make up the bulk of Venezuelan exports.

People and Lifestyle

A Mixed People and a Diverse Community

Venezuela has a population of nearly 24 million. More than two-thirds are mestizos, or people of mixed European and Amerindian or African ancestry, while about 20 percent of Venezuelans are of European descent, and about 10 percent are of African descent. Less than 2 percent of Venezuelans are Amerindian. Most European Venezuelans have Spanish roots, while others have either Italian, Portuguese, or German ancestors.

The Venezuelan population is young, with more than 55 percent of the country's people under twenty-five years of age. Over 95 percent of Venezuelans are under age sixty-five, and within this group, there are slightly more men than women. Venezuelan women, however, tend to outlive men. Among Venezuelans aged sixty-five and older, there are significantly more women than men. In 2001, figures showed that Venezuelan men live for an average of seventy years, while women live for an average of seventy-six and a half years.

HEALTH IN VENEZUELA
Many Venezuelan children, especially those from low-income families or rural areas, do not receive adequate medical care. The states of Apure, Portuguesa, Amazonas, and Delta Amacuro have the most people living in extreme poverty.
(A Closer Look, page 52)

Below: Excluding Venezuelans aged sixty-five and older, the Venezuelan population has slightly more men than women.

Ethnicity, Class, and Affluence

Spanish colonial Venezuela was a class conscious society and only two social classes — upper and lower — were recognized. Members of the upper class were called *gente decente* (HEN-teh deh-SEHN-teh), or decent people, and were always white, while members of the lower class were called *gente cualquiera* (HEN-teh coo-ahl-kee-EH-rah), or common people, and included mestizos, Amerindians, and Africans. During the colonial years, a person's ethnicity predetermined whether the person belonged to the upper or lower class.

The Venezuelan national census has not identified Venezuelans by their ethnicity since 1926. As a result, figures relating to the ethnic composition of the Venezuelan population are no more than estimates. During the twentieth century, widespread blending of European, Amerindian, and African bloodlines through cross-cultural marriages created a more homogeneous society, with mestizos today accounting for an estimated 67 percent of the country's population. In recent years, however, the widening gap between Venezuela's rich and poor has caused divisions similar to the colonial class structure, except now it is based on level of affluence instead of ethnicity.

Above: **Only a tiny fraction of Venezuela's population can afford to live in this housing complex. Despite the country's prosperity in the 1990s, wealth is not evenly distributed among Venezuelans, and a growing majority of the population lives below the poverty line.**

Family Ties

Venezuelans hold their families close to their hearts, and it is heavily ingrained in Venezuelan culture that a person should always hold the welfare of their families above their own. The basic family unit in Venezuela usually consists of a married couple and their children, but many Venezuelans live with their extended families. Extended family units in Venezuela most commonly involve three generations, which extend from *abuelitos* (ah-bway-LEE-tohs), or grandparents, to grandchildren. Venezuelan children are taught to always respect their elders, all of whom, from abuelitos to parents to uncles and aunts, may play an active role in their upbringing. As Venezuela has been strongly influenced by Roman Catholicism and its traditions, many Venezuelan children also have godparents, who would have been appointed by the child's parents. A child's *madrina* (mah-DREE-nah), or godmother, and *padrino* (pah-DREE-noh), or godfather, are supposed to support his or her religious and moral education. Godparents are usually close and trusted friends of the family.

THE WOMEN OF VENEZUELA

In the past, Venezuelan culture has tended to uphold traditional gender roles. Husbands were usually dominant breadwinners, while wives were most often submissive homemakers. In recent years, however, Venezuelan women have gradually broken away from tradition and taken on more visible roles in Venezuelan society. Education is key in allowing women these opportunities (*above*).
(*A Closer Look, page 72*)

Left: **A young mother and her two children go on an outing in the shopping district of Caracas.**

Urban and Rural Life

The vast majority of Venezuelans — more than 75 percent — live in cities. Venezuela's four largest cities are Caracas, Maracaibo, Valencia, and Barquisimeto. These four cities combined are home to more than 40 percent of Venezuelans. Ciudad Guayana, Maracay, and Petare are Venezuela's other larger cities, with populations ranging between 500,000 and a million people.

Between 1940 and 1970, Venezuela experienced rapid urbanization. The country's lucrative oil industry attracted waves of migrants from the rural areas to the urban areas. Venezuela's urban population doubled by 1949, and the country's rural to urban migration trend slowed only slightly throughout the 1950s. As a result, many Venezuelan cities, especially Caracas, suffered major housing shortages. The government attempted to alleviate the situation by spending large sums of money on public housing, but even the increased supply still fell far short of demand. As a result, *ranchos* (RAHN-chohs), or shantytowns, began to mushroom on the hilly outskirts of Venezuela's major cities. Over time the government came to accept these unplanned housing developments and even provided funds to convert some of the older ranchos into permanent housing structures.

Above: **The first ranchos were makeshift shelters and did not have water, electricity, or sewer systems. Today, some ranchos, such as these in Caracas, have access to utilities.**

RURAL RANCHOS

Rural ranchos tend to lack modern amenities, such as electricity and running water. Often, kerosene lamps are used to provide light and warmth, while water has to be carried from nearby streams or wells. Beds are luxuries in rural ranchos, where most residents sleep in hammocks.

Education

The Venezuelan education system consists of three main levels: elementary school, secondary school, and higher education. Venezuelan elementary school spans nine years and provides Educación Basica, or basic education, to all Venezuelans between the ages of six and fourteen. Educación Basica is compulsory and free, and the country has about 20,000 elementary schools. Spanish is the language of instruction.

Upon completing basic education, students can choose to enter one of two types of secondary, or high, schools: diversified or specialized. Specialized secondary school provides Educación Media Profesional, which is a three-year vocational course. Students pursuing specialized secondary education can choose from a range of technical, farming, or nursing courses. Diversified secondary school, on the other hand, provides Educación Media Diversificada, which is a two-year course that prepares students for higher education in the subjects they have chosen. Venezuela has more than 2,000 secondary schools.

Below: **These students are learning to think creatively using methods devised by Dr. Edward de Bono (1933–), who is famous for his theories on "lateral thinking." Venezuelan law requires all schoolchildren to spend one hour a week exploring de Bono's methods. Venezuela has a literacy rate of over 91 percent. Slightly more men than women are able to read and write.**

Y Qué Tengo qué Decírle a la Universidad como Artículo Primero como Función Esencial de su Vida ( )Le Tengo que Decir Que se Pinte de Mulato No Sólo Entre Los Alumnos, si no También Entre Los Profesores: que se Pinte De Obrero y De Campesino, Que se Pinte De Pueblo Porque La Universid No es el Patrimonio de NADIE Y Pertenece AL Pueblo...

Higher Education

Between the late 1950s and the early 1980s, strong encouragement from the Venezuelan government led to a sharp increase in the number and types of institutions providing post-secondary education. Today, Venezuela has about thirty colleges and universities, as well as more than one hundred other institutes of higher learning. Non-university courses tend to last between two and a half and three years, while university courses, depending on the field, take between four to six years to complete.

Caracas is the country's center of higher education, with several major universities located within the capital's territory. Universidad Central de Venezuela (Central University of Venezuela), Universidad Nacional Abierta (National Open University), and Universidad Simón Bolívar (Simón Bolívar University) are among the most respected institutions. Outside of Caracas, some other Venezuelan states are also home to respected universities, including Universidad de Zulia (University of Zulia) and Universidad de Carabobo (University of Carabobo).

Above: Painted on the outer wall of the Universidad Central de Venezuela in Caracas, this mural dominates the view from a metro, or subway, exit near the university. The right half of the mural is a portrait of Ernesto Guevara (1928–1967), or Che Guevara. A famous revolutionary, Guevara believed in the power of the people. The other half of the mural bears a message urging that education should be for all and not reserved for only the social elite.

Religion

Ninety-six percent of Venezuelans identify themselves as Roman Catholic, but far fewer are known to actively practice the religion. Of the remaining 4 percent of Venezuelans, about half are Protestants, while the other half consists of Jews, Muslims, and believers in various traditional Amerindian or African beliefs. Venezuela has fifteen synagogues and one mosque.

Protestantism appears to be the fastest-growing religion in Venezuela today. Since the 1980s, evangelical denominations, including Lutherans and Baptists, have been converting more and more Venezuelans from Roman Catholicism to Protestantism. Some have estimated that the number of Venezuelan Protestants has increased fourfold since 1981.

Venezuelan Jews

Venezuela's fifteen synagogues are located in the cities of Caracas, Maracaibo, Porlamar, Valencia, Maracay, and Puerto La Cruz. About half of Venezuela's Jewish population lives in

EARLY CATHOLIC MISSIONARIES

In the seventeenth and eighteenth centuries, Roman Catholic clergy arrived in Venezuela in large numbers. Their main goal was to convert the indigenous people to Christianity.

(*A Closer Look, page 50*)

THE VIRGIN OF COROMOTO

Located about 250 miles (402 km) southwest of Caracas, the Virgin of Coromoto cathedral is special to devout Venezuelan Roman Catholics. The cathedral stands on the site where many Venezuelans believe the Virgin Mary appeared to an Amerindian chief in the seventeenth century. Pope John Paul II blessed the cathedral in 1996.

Left: Built in 1994, the Al Ibrahim Mosque in Caracas is the only mosque in Venezuela.

Left: The Santa Capilla church in Caracas was declared a basilica in 1928. Basilicas are Roman Catholic churches that have been given special religious status by the pope.

THE CULT OF MARÍA LIONZA

The cult of María Lionza is a folk religion that combines elements of Amerindian beliefs, African voodoo, and Christianity. The religious rites of the cult have been described as resembling witchcraft. Located in the state of Yaracuy, the Montanas de Sorte, or Sorte Mountains, which are part of the Costal Cordillera, are considered sacred by the cult's followers, who believe that María Lionza lives there. Little is known about María Lionza, but legend has it that she was a beautiful Amerindian girl, who disappeared into the forest and never again emerged. Her worshipers regard her as the goddess of all things natural, including forests and wild animals. Followers of the cult were traditionally from the northwestern parts of Venezuela but today come from all over the country.

Caracas. Another significant concentration of Jews is in Maracaibo. The Venezuelan Jewish community has, over the years, made serious efforts to uphold Jewish culture, beliefs, and values in the country. In Venezuela, over 70 percent of school-age Jews attend Jewish schools, which include preschool, elementary, and secondary curricula. Jewish higher education is also available at the Higher Institute of Jewish Studies and the Yeshiva Guedola de Venezuela. *Nuevo Mundo Israelita*, a weekly newspaper, and *Shalom,* a weekly radio program, keeps Venezuela's Jewish community informed and connected.

Language and Literature

Spanish and Other Languages

Spanish, Venezuela's official language, was introduced by the colonists, who arrived in the sixteenth century. More and more Venezuelans today are learning English as a second language. In addition to Arabic, Chinese, and German, which are spoken by the country's respective minority groups, over thirty languages are spoken by Venezuela's indigenous peoples.

Pemón, Piaroa, Warao, Wayuu, and Yanomamö are some of the more commonly spoken indigenous languages in Venezuela. In fact, some Venezuelan Amerindians speak only their native tongues because they live in deeply remote areas, such as the Amazonian forests, where Spanish is not the predominant language. Several indigenous languages, such as Akawaio, Arawak, Arutani, Baré, Mapoyo, Paraujano, Sapé, and Tunebo, however, are on the verge of becoming extinct. Most of these are languages of either the Arawak or Carib peoples. Baniva and Yavitero, both of which originated from the Arawak people, have already become extinct.

Above: **A man in Caracas' Plaza Bolívar reads about Hugo Chavez's victory in the 1998 presidential elections.**

Left: **Newsstands in Caracas commonly carry an extensive range of publications.**

Left: **Arturo Uslar Pietri (1906–2001) is one of Venezuela's best-loved authors. In 1991, he won the Rómulo Gallegos Prize for Literature for his novel** *Una Visita en el tiempo,* **or** *A Visit in Time.*

Literature

During the Spanish colonial years, most Venezuelan literature was written in the form of chronicles or poetry. Venezuelan literature only began to form its own identity in the nineteenth century, when two revolutionary movements — the country's struggle for independence and the rise of Romanticism in the mid-1800s — injected creative vigor into the country's literary scene.

Venezuela's struggle for independence inspired much passionate literature. The country's influential authors include Simón Bolívar, Francisco de Miranda, and Andrés Bello, who was Bolívar's tutor. *Peonia* (1890) by Manuel Romero García (1861–1917) has come to be known as the definitive text of Venezuelan Romanticism. *Venezuela Heroica* (1881) and *Biografia de José Félix Ribas* (1859) by Eduardo Blanco (1810–1912) and Juan Vicente González (1810–1866), respectively, both of whom were heavily influenced by Bolívar's works, are highly respected books.

During the twentieth century, Venezuelan literature truly flourished. While some authors continued to be inspired by local and regional politics, others sought to follow European or North American literary trends. Today, Venezuelan literature is diverse and unique because of its multiethnic heritage, which includes European, Amerindian, African, and Caribbean experiences.

A LEGENDARY POET

Born in 1918, Ana Enriqueta Terán is famous for her moving poetry both in and out of Venezuela. She was awarded the country's highest literary honor, the Premio Nacional de Literatura, or the National Prize for Literature, in 1989. Today, Enriqueta Terán is writing her autobiography, which will only be published after she dies.

Arts

Venezuela's diverse ethnic heritage, with European, Caribbean, African, and Amerindian roots, has led to the birth of a wide range of art forms. Many Venezuelan artists have creatively combined two or more ethnic influences in their artistic pursuits, which include music, dance, theater, and visual art.

Painting and Sculpture

Before the Spanish arrived, artwork in Venezuela included rock carving, cave painting, and pottery. During the colonial years, artistic expression in Venezuela was heavily censored by the Roman Catholic Church and, thus, tended to feature only religious figures or scenes. Following its declaration of independence, Venezuela produced a number of famous painters, such as Manuel Cabré (1890–1984), Hector Poleo (1918–1989), and Martín Továr y Továr (1827–1902). Továr's best-known work is found on the ceiling of the Capitolio Nacional. His mural depicts Simón Bolívar's victory at the Battle of Carabobo.

HERMIT PAINTER

Nicknamed the "Hermit of Macuto," Armando Reverón (1889–1954) refused to converse or interact with anybody apart from his wife and one close friend, who also modeled for some of his paintings. Macuto is a tiny coastal town just north of Caracas.

Below: An artist in Plaza Bolívar paints his impression of the square on a canvas. Plaza Bolívar is widely regarded as the heart of colonial Caracas.

In recent decades, kinetic art has been a rapidly developing art form in Venezuela. Kinetic art incorporates movement, whether real or perceived, into sculptures. Famous Venezuelan kinetic artists include Jesús Soto (1923–), Carlos Cruz-Díez (1923–), and Alejandro Otero (1921–). Many of Soto's works are displayed outside prominent buildings in Caracas. Otero is famous for *La abra solar*, which involves a beautifully intricate, metallic cross that moves and sways when there is wind.

Above: **An installation of kinetic art by Jesús Soto hangs outside this building in Caracas. The Museo Jesús Soto, or Jesús Soto Museum, is located in Ciudad Bolívar, where Soto was born. Opened in 1973, the museum showcases many of Soto's admired works.**

Handicrafts

Folk art in Venezuela varies from region to region and is often closely related to the cultures and lifestyles of the artisans. The country's best saddles and ropes, for example, are made by the *Llanero* (yah-NEH-roh), or the cowboys of the Llanos in central Venezuela. The Llanero are also famous for making fine musical instruments. The *Guayanés* (goo-ah-yah-NEHS), who reside in the Amazonian rain forests, are skilled makers of hammocks and canoes, while the friendly *Andinos* (ahn-DEE-nohs), or people of the Andes, whose towns and villages typically date back to Spanish colonial times, produce high-quality pottery.

Music

Since the fall of Spanish colonial rule in the country, unique brands of Venezuelan folk music combining Spanish, African, and Amerindian rhythms have evolved. On the country's northeastern coast, the presence of African beats in the local music is unmistakable. Venezuela's northeastern coast had been a key center for the colonial slave trade, which explains the prominence of African musical influences in the region. *Un Solo Pueblo*, or One People, is a popular, Venezuelan musical group that is famous for combining the folk music of the Llanos with African rhythms. Gaita is a traditional style of music originating from the state of Zulia. Gaita combines improvised vocals, which must rhyme, with the sounds of the *cuatro* (coo-AH-troh), a small, four-stringed guitar, and maracas, or a pair of gourd-shaped rattles. Today, gaita is mainly identified in Venezuela as traditional Christmas music, but it is also played at various festivals throughout the year.

JOROPO: THE NATIONAL DANCE

Much like other dances favored by Venezuelans, the *joropo* (hoh-ROH-poh) is festive, energetic, and passionate.
(A Closer Look, page 54)

OSCAR D'LEON: A SALSA SENSATION

Oscar D'Leon is a salsa legend in Venezuela. His silky vocals and talent for improvisation has made him a Latin superstar.
(A Closer Look, page 60)

Below: A maker of various stringed instruments holds up a completed cuatro.

Above: **Many old houses in Venezuela, such as these in central Maracaibo, have been painstakingly restored and painted with bright colors.**

Architecture

Spanish-style buildings still standing in Venezuela today may appear to pale in comparison to the grander colonial structures found in neighboring countries such as Peru, Colombia, and Ecuador. The development of Venezuela's modern architecture, however, has been spectacular. Venezuelan architecture was lifted to new heights with the onset of Modernism, as well as the newfound wealth from the country's mid-twentieth century oil boom. Many older parts of Caracas also underwent renovation and expansion during the oil boom.

Honored as the "Master of Modern Venezuelan Architecture," Carlos Raúl Villanueva (1900–1975) designed many of Venezuela's magnificent contemporary structures. La Ciudad de Universidad de Caracas, or the University City of the University of Caracas, was probably Villanueva's greatest accomplishment. Beginning in 1944, the enormous complex took sixteen years to complete. Today, the premises are utilized by thousands of students and include a concert hall and a sports complex among numerous other facilities. The University City is considered a classic piece of twentieth-century architecture.

VALENCIA: OLD CITY, NEW CITY

Valencia is home to many Spanish-style colonial buildings that lend the city an old-world charm. Valencia is Venezuela's fourth-largest city and an important commercial center.

(A Closer Look, page 70)

Leisure and Festivals

Venezuelans spend a lot of their free time with their families, whether at home or out. Venezuelans especially love to eat out, so much so that no other South American city has as many restaurants per person as Caracas. Families or groups of friends often prefer to catch up with each other over a meal at a restaurant rather than at home.

Venezuelan families also enjoy going to the movies. Most movies shown in the country are imported, foreign-language films subtitled in Spanish. Venezuela's own filmmaking industry is underdeveloped and only makes a few movies each year. With a history that dates back to the late eighteenth century, Venezuelan theater possesses greater local flavor, which some Venezuelans prefer. Caracas is also home to a great number of art galleries and museums, including Museo de Bellas Artes (Museum of Fine Art), Museo del Arte Colonial (Museum of Colonial Art), Museo de Ciencias Naturales (Museum of Natural

Below: **Bullfights and rodeos are favorite traditional spectator events in Venezuela. Bullfights are mostly organized during special holidays and festivals. Numerous cities, including Valencia, Mérida, Barquismeto, and Barcelona, maintain bullfighting rings.**

Above: **Ecotourists take in the sights as they travel down a tributary of the Orinoco River.**

Sciences), and Museo Bolívar (Bolívar Museum). As dancing is a strong part of Venezuelan culture, many adult Venezuelans enjoy dancing in nightclubs.

The country's diverse and scenic landscapes provide Venezuelans with many opportunities for relaxing getaways and nature-related recreational activities, such as ecotourism, birdwatching, and caving. Birdwatchers in Venezuela have reported sighting numerous species of kites, doves, parrots, swifts, hummingbirds, tanagers, woodpeckers, and vultures, including the majestic Andean condor. The Orinoco Delta, which is the swampy coastal area in northeastern Venezuela where the Orinoco River empties into the Atlantic Ocean, is home to herons, storks, ducks, and cranes, as well as a huge number of ibises.

Apart from exploring the country's lush and serene highlands, many Venezuelans also love relaxing at the beach. Located about 109 miles (176 km) north of Caracas, the Islas Los Roques, or the Los Roques Islands, have some of the finest beaches on Earth. The islands were declared a national park in 1972.

CAVING

Several hundred caves exist in Venezuela, but most caving enthusiasts aim to visit the Cueva del Guacharo, or Guacharo Cave. Located in Caripe, which is a small town just northwest of the city of Caripito, the Guacharo Cave is Venezuela's longest cave.

Left: Venezuelans who love watersports such as windsurfing, water skiing, diving, and snorkeling can use the country's generous Caribbean coastline and numerous offshore islands.

Sports

Venezuelans take part in a phenomenal number of sports, ranging from adventure sports to martial arts to ball games, including baseball, basketball, and rugby.

With over forty national parks and numerous nature reserves, Venezuela's plentiful scenic landscapes provide the ideal surroundings for a variety of adventure sports, such as hiking, rock climbing, mountain biking, hang gliding, horseback riding, kayaking, and diving. Venezuelans typically visit the Andes mountains or the Guiana Highlands to hike, rock climb, and mountain bike. Peninsula de Paraguaná, or Paraguaná Peninsula, which extends from the country's northwestern coast, and Margarita Island, which lies off the country's northeastern coast, are often crowded with enthusiasts of various watersports. With ecotourism becoming increasingly popular among Venezuelans and international tourists, the Venezuelan government has made efforts to protect the country's rich wildlife. Hunting for game is prohibited by law, although sport fishing is allowed in certain areas, provided special permits have been obtained.

LAWN BOWLING

Bolas criollas (BOH-lahs cree-OH-yahs), or lawn bowling, has a small but loyal following in Venezuela. The game can be played between two individuals or two teams. Players roll thick, wooden discs toward a smaller ball, called a jack, placed at the end of a rink. A rink is a marked section of lawn that measures 18 by 21 feet (5.5 by 6.4 m). The intent of the game is to roll the wooden discs so that they stop as close to the jack as possible without touching it. With each subsequent roll, players are also supposed to try to knock their opponents' discs out of place while avoiding the jack. The game ends when contact has been made with the jack. The player or the team of the player who caused the jack to move loses the game.

Baseball

Although soccer is a favorite sport in most South American countries, Venezuela's national sport is, in fact, baseball. The sport first gained mass popularity in the country in the early twentieth century, when lots of North American professionals arrived to work in the Venezuelan oil industry. By the mid-1900s, baseball became firmly established in the Venezuelan sporting scene with the birth of the country's first professional league.

Most Venezuelan cities have their own baseball diamonds and stadiums, and the country has a winter league. Every year, eight teams from various parts of the country play against each other in the winter league, which begins in October and lasts for four months. The winning team, in turn, represents the country in the Serie del Caribe, or the Caribbean Series, which is a regional competition held every February and involves teams from Venezuela, Mexico, Puerto Rico, and the Dominican Republic. In 2002, the series was hosted by Venezuela, and the games were played in Caracas.

Below: **Cesar Isturiz (*left*) of Venezuela's Magallanes Navegantes slides on to second base as D'Angelo Jimenez (*right*) of the Dominican Republic's Tigres de Licey tries to tag him. The two teams were competing in the 2002 Caribbean Series.**

Festivals

Because so many Venezuelans are Roman Catholic, many of the country's festivals and holidays are related to their religion. Venezuelans also celebrate a number of secular holidays, which include the anniversary of the momentous victory at the Battle of Carabobo in 1821 (June 24), Independence Day (July 5), Simón Bolívar's birthday (July 24), and Día de la Raza (October 12). Día de la Raza, which translates literally into "Day of the Race," is also known as Columbus Day. This holiday celebrates the Hispanic heritage of the peoples of Latin American countries.

Some Venezuelan states and villages honor their respective patron saints with an annual regional festival. Día de San Juan, or Day of Saint John, is one such festival and is celebrated every June by the people of Barlovento, a region in the state of Miranda. Honoring Saint John and lasting three days, the festival involves much feasting and, more importantly, dancing to infectious drumbeats played by the region's people. Products of much African influence, the drumming and dances of Barlovento are performed for numerous festivals celebrated throughout the year.

In the state of Mérida, La Paradura del Niño, or the Parade of the Child, is held every January. Locals carry a figure of the baby Jesus through the streets in a festive procession celebrating the birth of Christ.

Some religious festivals such as La Cruz de Mayo, or the Cross of May, and Semana Santa, or Holy Week, are celebrated nationwide. During La Cruz de Mayo, Venezuelans customarily decorate large crosses with beautiful flowers and sing and pray in the act of worshipping the Holy Cross. Holy Week consists of the days before the crucifixion of Christ and ends with Easter Sunday. Venezuelans from different parts of the country observe Holy Week differently, but, throughout the country, an effigy of Judas Iscariot, who, according to the Bible, betrayed Jesus, is always burnt to mark the week's end.

Carnival is one of the most elaborately celebrated events in Venezuela and can fall in either February or March. Carnival is always celebrated on the Tuesday before Ash Wednesday, and in Venezuela, the Monday before Carnival is also a holiday. In the larger cities, brightly colored costumes, elaborate floats, and noisy street parades are typical during Carnival.

Above: **Venezuelans celebrating Carnival fill the streets dressed in colorful clothes and wearing equally colorful masks. Dancing is also a must, and lively, upbeat tunes are played throughout the day.**

Food

Combining a diverse ethnic heritage with a wide variety of local produce, meats, and the plentiful seafood from the Caribbean waters has led to the invention of some uniquely Venezuelan dishes. A quintessentially Venezuelan food is the *arepa* (ah-REH-pah), which is a piece of cooked dough made from corn flour, water, and salt. Venezuelans eat arepas in much the same way people of other cultures eat bread. Arepas can be eaten fresh and plain or stuffed with various kinds of fillings. In the morning, for example, arepas are customarily stuffed with *perico* (peh-REE-koh), or scrambled eggs tossed with tomatoes and onions. Arepas are also known to be stuffed with salad, cheese, and meats, such as beef, chicken, ham, and sausage.

Venezuela's national dish, *Pabellón Criollo* (pah-beh-YOHN cree-OH-yoh), is a stew made from shredded beef. It is typically eaten with rice, black beans, and fried plantains. Plantains are similar to bananas and grow on trees, which are commonly found in the tropics.

Below: To make arepas, the dough mixture, which consists of corn flour, water, and salt, is first divided and molded into round disks. In a lightly greased pan, the disks are fried until a crust has formed on both sides. The half-cooked arepas are then baked or grilled until done. Makers of arepas tap an arepa's surface to check if it is done. If the tapping produces a hollow sound, then the arepa is done and ready to be eaten.

Above: **Venezuelans enjoy lunch at this sidewalk café in the Sabana Grande district of Caracas.**

A well-loved, traditional Venezuelan dish is *hallaca* (ah-YAH-kah). Considered a local delicacy by some, hallaca is a rich mixture of cornmeal, beef, pork, chicken, green peppers, tomatoes, onions, garlic, olives, raisins, and various herbs and spices. The mixture is wrapped in plantain leaves and then steamed or boiled in water. Hallaca takes a few days to prepare and is usually eaten during the Christmas season.

Venezuela is blessed with a breathtaking variety of exotic, tropical fruits, such as pineapple, papaya, guava, mango, and coconut. Apart from being eaten fresh, the fruits are also juiced or made into delicious milkshakes, or *merengada* (meh-rehn-GAH-dah). Made from rice starch, milk, vanilla, and sugar, *chicha de arroz* (CHEE-chah deh ah-ROHS) is another delectable sweet treat. Venezuelans also enjoy a special kind of lemonade, called *papelon con limon* (pah-peh-LOHN kohn lee-MOHN), that is sweetened with raw sugar instead of refined sugar.

Venezuelan coffee is another local treat. Intensely aromatic and with a taste that is mild, mellow, and delicate, Venezuelan coffee has been described as unique in the Americas.

A CLOSER LOOK AT VENEZUELA

Modern Venezuelans generally put little emphasis on racial distinctions and, instead, prefer to celebrate the mixed heritage that they each embody and makes Venezuelan culture a unique experience. Venezuela also has beautiful landscapes, which range from magnificent table mountains to pristine Caribbean beaches to lush Amazonian rain forests. In recent years, serious efforts have been made by both the government and large corporations to protect Venezuela's natural treasures. With cities nearly as diverse as its natural landscapes, Venezuela is home to many

Opposite: **Located in La Gran Sabana, the Salto Aponguao, or Aponguao Falls, is 344 feet (105 m) high.**

types of architecture, vibrant traditions in music and dance, and an oil industry with a productive past and potentially fruitful future. The heart of Caracas, Venezuela's capital city and political and business center, is a mesh of futuristic skyscrapers and interweaving freeways. The city of Valencia, on the other hand, while modern, is better known for its large number of colonial buildings. From joropo, the country's national dance, to its international salsa music stars, the country produces distinctive forms of entertainment. At the beginning of the twenty-first century, Venezuela was fraught with economic problems, despite having some of the world's largest reserves of oil.

Above: **A massive granite formation, the Kukenan "table mountain" in La Gran Sabana, is a magnificent sight.**

Amerindians in Venezuela

Although less than 2 percent of Venezuelans are Amerindian, they divide into over thirty ethnic groups. Venezuelan Amerindians live mostly in the country's southern and eastern regions. At over 40 percent of the population, the state of Amazonas has the highest number of Amerindians, of whom the Piaroa and Yanomami peoples form a majority. The Waraos dominate the Orinoco Delta in northeastern Venezuela, while the Pemón concentrate in southeastern Venezuela, near the country's border with Guyana. The Yukpa and Wayuu peoples, who generally reside in the country's northwest, form small minority groups within the larger Venezuelan Amerindian population.

The Yanomamis

First encountered in the 1920s, the Yanomamis lived virtually untouched by external influences for the next fifty years until a gold rush attracted waves of miners into their homeland — an area of rain forest that straddles southern Venezuela and northern

INDIGENOUS RIGHTS

Before 1999, when Venezuela's constitution was revised, the country's laws on indigenous rights were the most unprogressive in Latin America. Today, Amazonas is represented by a governor and three mayors, all of whom are of indigenous descent and were popularly elected — something unprecedented in Venezuelan history.

YANOMAMI LANGUAGES

The Yanomami people speak as many as four languages — Yanomamö and three dialects. The dialects are Parima, or eastern Yanomami; Padamo-Orinoco, or western Yanomami; and Kobali, or Cobari. Kobali is sometimes referred to as Cobariwa.

Left: Yanomami children begin training for various hunting skills, including climbing, from a very young age.

44

Brazil. Since the miners arrived, thousands of Yanomamis have
perished, whether from bloody clashes with the miners over
territorial trespasses; foreign diseases, such as tuberculosis and
measles, against which the Yanomamis have no immunity; or
malnutrition. Mining operations have contaminated the area's
vital water sources with mercury, while the airplanes used by the
miners to enter and leave the remote area have scared away many
of the animals that the Yanomamis traditionally hunt for food.
Today, only about 12,000 Yanomamis survive in Venezuela.

The Waraos

With a population of over 20,000, the Waraos are one of the larger
Amerindian groups in Venezuela, where they have dominated the
Orinoco Delta for over 3,000 years. In the late twentieth century,
however, intensive oil-drilling operations in the region destroyed
the natural environment and greatly interfered with the
traditional Warao way of life. Inevitable oil leaks and accidental
oil spills have turned more and more sources of freshwater into
toxic streams. As a result, the Waraos are deprived of not only
clean drinking water, but also fish and shellfish, which they have
always relied on for food. Today, many Waraos are forced to
accept government handouts or purchase their food.

WARAO TRAGEDIES

By 1997, Isla de Plata,
or Silver Island, had sunk
after less than two years
of drilling in the oil fields
surrounding the island.
Isla de Plata was formerly
the home of about 200
Warao Indians.

An even greater
tragedy occurred in 1967,
when one of the Orinoco
River's major tributaries
was suddenly closed. The
resulting stagnant waters
led to a malaria epidemic
that claimed about 6,000
Warao lives.

Blessed with "Black Gold"

After the discovery of Venezuela's first major oil field — La Rosa — in 1922, the country's oil industry developed at a remarkable speed and brought economic prosperity unknown to any other South American country. When oil prices soared in the 1970s, Venezuela had the highest income per capita in South America.

Venezuela's largest known oil reserves are located in the lowland areas surrounding Lake Maracaibo and underneath the lake itself. Oil reserves have also been discovered in the Llanos, the Orinoco Delta, and off the country's Caribbean shore. At the end of the twentieth century, Venezuela was producing about 3.5 million barrels of crude oil a day and was the world's fourth-largest producer of oil.

Before President Hugo Chavez's radical economic reform policies took effect in 2001, Petróleos de Venezuela, S. A. (PDVSA) was the world's forty-fifth-largest company and was recognized as one of Latin America's best run companies. PDVSA maintained world-class operational efficiency and financial practices. Since the introduction of Chavez's policies, however, the government-

OPEC MEMBER

In 1960, Venezuela, Iran, Iraq, Kuwait, and Saudi Arabia founded the Organization of Petroleum Exporting Countries (OPEC).

The first OPEC countries came together in response to one-sided decisions by British Petroleum (BP) in 1959 and Standard Oil of New Jersey (present-day ExxonMobil) in 1960 to cut oil prices, which disadvantaged countries that had economies heavily reliant on oil.

Left: The simple facade of PDVSA's main office building in Caracas does not reflect the great wealth that the company controls. Founded in 1975, PDVSA has since expanded its interests to include other sources of energy, such as natural gas, Orimulsion, and coal.

owned and government-run monopoly's total net profits fell steadily from more than U.S. $7 billion in 2000 to about U.S. $4 billion in 2001 to U.S. $2 billion in 2002.

Alternative Energy Sources

Apart from crude oil, Venzuela also has considerable reserves of natural bitumen and liquid natural gas (LNG). In 2000, the country produced more than 1,450 billion cubic feet (41,035 million cubic meters) of LNG. According to PDVSA, Venezuela has about 148 trillion cubic feet (4.2 trillion cubic meters) of LNG, or about 30 percent of known reserves in South America.

Mixing natural bitumen with water produces a special type of fossil fuel, which has been branded Orimulsion. Orimulsion is being used to power electric generators in countries such as Canada, China, Singapore, Japan, Italy, and Germany. Venezuela's natural bitumen reserves are estimated at 46 billion tons (42 billion metric tons), which some experts claim can last well into the twenty-second century.

Above: Venezuela's oil industry was producing 3.9 million barrels of crude oil a day before its rapid deterioration at the beginning of the twenty-first century. The infrastructure PDVSA had built to support the large volume of oil exports included some 20,000 active oil wells, 3,728 miles (6,000 km) of oil pipelines, and about 300 oil fields.

The Capital City of Caracas

With a population of nearly 5 million, the Metropolitan Area of Greater Caracas was formed when the original boundaries of the city of Caracas were extended to include the neighboring towns of Libertador, Chacao, Sucre, Baruta, and El Hatillo. Greater Caracas is also a site of many sharp contrasts. The metropolitan area is as advanced as it is underdeveloped, as plainly luxurious as it is violently crime-ridden, and as chic as it is downright dirty.

Nestled in a valley of the towering Avila mountains, which are part of the Coastal Cordillera, central Caracas overlooks the Caribbean Sea. It is a tightly packed area of ultramodern skyscrapers and crisscrossing freeways. Looking up or out from some parts of the capital city is breathtakingly picturesque. Outside the city's modern center, however, are views far less pleasing to the eye. Ranchos, or shantytowns, crowd the city's surrounding inclines. Stacked to precarious heights, these homes for the poor form an assembly of tin roofs and uneven concrete.

Below: **Caracas was once nicknamed the "City of Red Roofs" because of the color of the roof tiles used on many colonial houses and structures. Today, the skyline of Caracas is dominated by numerous imposing gray skyscrapers.**

Ranchos house about one-third of the metropolitan area's population. The prevailing poverty and intense overcrowding, however, has not prevented Caracas from becoming one of South America's more hip and cosmopolitan cities.

Since it was founded, Caracas has been heavily damaged by a number of earthquakes, including the 1812 disaster that destroyed 90 percent of the city and killed 10,000 people. The city underwent extensive renovation in the 1950s and the 1970s, as a result of the wealth generated by the oil boom. A significant number of colonial buildings, however, remain. Plaza Bolívar, which is marked by a magnificent statue of Simón Bolívar on a horse, is at the heart of colonial Caracas. The plaza is surrounded by some of Venezuela's major historical landmarks, such as Capitolio Nacional and Concejo Municipal. Venezuelan congress meetings are still held in the Capitolio Nacional, which is easily identifiable by its distinctive golden dome. Concejo Municipal serves as a town hall. It is where the country's declaration of independence was written nearly two centuries ago. The building that houses the Museo de Arte Colonial, or Museum of Colonial Art, is the grand colonial home, called Quinta de Anauco, where Bolívar spent his last night in Venezuela.

Above: **Although the city is serviced by a clean and efficient metro, or subway, system, Caracas still suffers from intense traffic congestion. Built in the 1970s, multitiered traffic junctions affectionately known as the "spider" and the "octopus" have long been a part of the Caracas cityscape but have done little to alleviate the problem they were designed to resolve. Delays have come to be accepted as an inevitable part of life in Caracas.**

Early Catholic Missionaries

Religion, specifically Roman Catholicism, played a significant role in the colonization of Venezuela, as well as other Latin American countries. While the colonists who worked directly for the Spanish Crown were preoccupied with enslaving the Amerindians and exploiting the riches of the land, the early Catholic missionaries, who also arrived from Spain, had a different motivation.

The Capuchins, or an order of Franciscan friars that observes vows of poverty and austerity, were among the earliest Catholic missionaries to settle in Venezuela. Many settlements built in the harsh and rural parts of Venezuela, such as the city of San Carlos (founded in 1678), were the fruits of their determined labor. Apart from converting Amerindians to Roman Catholicism, the Capuchins also successfully ran settlements that not only became self-sufficient, but also prospered from their agricultural successes.

LOBBYING FOR HUMAN RIGHTS

According to some historians of Roman Catholicism, the early clergy were always mindful of the need to defend the indigenous peoples of Venezuela, as well as the rest of Latin America, from the colonists. The clergy, these historians suggest, were the first people to lobby for a set of laws, called leyes de las Indias, that pledged peaceful coexistence with the Amerindians in the process of colonization.

Left: This illustration is an artist's impression of Roman Catholic missionaries making contact with Amerindians natives in the sixteenth century.

The presence of Roman Catholic missionaries in colonial Venezuela reached its height in the seventeenth and eighteenth centuries, when the missionaries came to dominate Venezuela's Llanos and Maracaibo regions. The missionaries who came later were mostly Franciscans and Dominicans. Unlike the Capuchins, they were less interested in educating the Amerindians about the ideas and practices of Western civilization than they were in converting them — sometimes forcibly — to Christianity.

For the Amerindians, converting to Christianity meant abandoning animistic beliefs and values, practices and rituals that were supported by a centuries-old heritage. The Christian missionaries also insisted that the Amerindians accept a host of doctrines, such as the holy sacraments, salvation, heaven and hell, the Virgin Mary and saints, and the crucified Christ, that were new and unusual to them. The Spanish Inquisition (1478–1834) eventually destroyed Venezuela's native religious cultures. Temples of the indigenous peoples were burned and the idols they worshiped were destroyed because the Spanish colonists viewed them as products of the devil.

Above: **In this painting, missionaries are converting native Amerindians to Christianity in the late eighteenth and early nineteenth centuries.**

Health in Venezuela

Health care is offered at both public and private institutions in Venezuela, and public health care is free. Compared to the rest of South America, Venezuela has an unusually high standard of health care. Since 1940, when Venezuelans lived for an average of forty-three years, the average life span in Venezuela has increased by more than 70 percent to reach seventy-three years.

In the years following World War II, the Venezuelan government played an active role in improving the general health of Venezuelans. Nationwide immunization programs, for example, have greatly reduced the number of deaths caused by contagious diseases such as tuberculosis, measles, malaria, and cholera. The Venezuelan government also actively monitors and maintains the quality of drinking water in the country. Chlorine, for example, is added to water reserves to kill harmful bacteria and other disease-spreading agents.

Below: Venezuelan health care reached enviable heights in the mid-1950s, when oil-wealth provided for great improvements in public services.

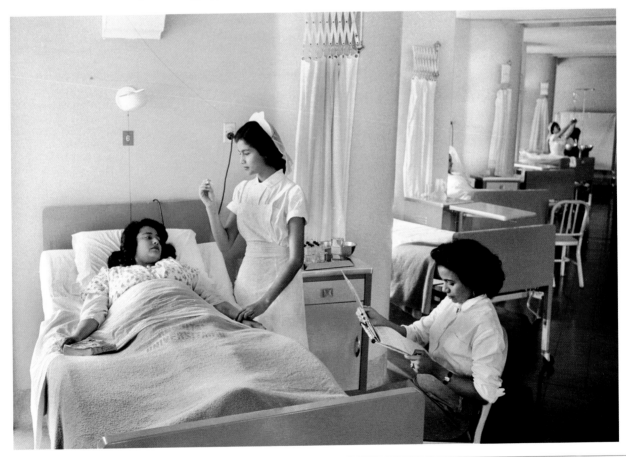

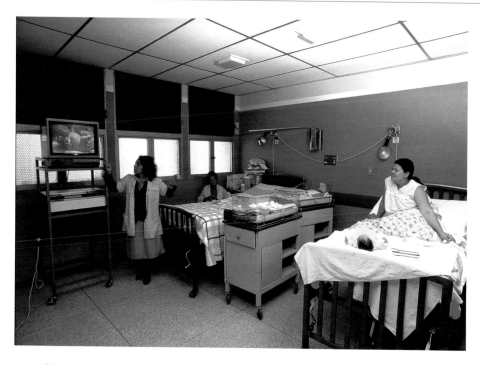

Left: **A social worker educates a first-time mother on how to take care of her newborn.**

Since the 1980s, when the Venezuelan economy was hit hard by the world slump in oil prices, however, health care has not been the target of much government spending. Today, many public hospitals and clinics are in dire need of repair and upgrading. Venezuelans with private insurance or those who can afford the high costs for treatment go to private hospitals, which are usually better equipped. Treatment is free at public hospitals and clinics, but prescription drugs cost money. Venezuelans, however, pay relatively little for prescription drugs because of heavy government subsidies.

In recent years, the number of Venezuelans who have tested positive for Human Immunodeficiency Virus (HIV) or who suffer from Acquired Immune Deficiency Syndrome (AIDS) has steadily increased, especially in the larger cities, such as Caracas, Mérida, and Maracaibo. In April 2001, the Supreme Court ruled that all Venezuelans suffering from HIV or AIDS are entitled to receive free treatment with antiretrovirals, which are the most effective drugs for HIV-positive and AIDS patients. Since then, the number of recipients of the free antiretroviral treatment has jumped from 2,000 to over 11,000. The program costs the Venezuelan government an estimated U.S. $1,000 a month for each patient. In 2002, the United Nations estimated that approximately 65,000 Venezuelans are either HIV-positive or suffering from AIDS.

Joropo: The National Dance

The joropo, a dance that originated in Venezuela's vast central plains, is performed by a man and a woman. Known by the same name, the music accompanying this dance involves improvised singing, a harp, a cuatro, and maracas. Although it comes from the cowboy culture to which only 10 percent of Venezuelans belong, the energetic joropo is the definitive Venezuelan folk dance. The Llaneros, or people of the plains, who created the joropo, descended from a mixture of Spanish, African, and Amerindian ancestry. Today, they continue to live on ranches and herd cattle for a living, as did their ancestors. The larger Venezuelan population regards the figure of the Llanos cowboy as representative of courage, strength, and independence.

When performing the joropo, the man's clothing usually includes a large sombrero and the woman's a long, wide, multicolored skirt. During the dance, the man typically holds his hands behind his back, while the woman dances around him. Sometimes the woman holds a scarf, which she works into the dance with special moves. Both dancers perform fast, sharply-

SALSA AND MERENGUE

Although the joropo is Venezuela's national dance, salsa and the merengue are more popular in the country. The salsa originated in Puerto Rico and the merengue comes from the Dominican Republic.

Left: The Llanos occupies about 115,800 square miles (300,000 square km), which is about one-third of Venezuela's area. From north to south, the length of the Llanos varies between 100 miles (161 km) in the east and 300 miles (483 km) in the west. The Llanos spreads over the states of Barinas, Portuguesa, Cojedes, Aragua, Guárico, and Apure.

Left: **On April 14, 2002, supporters of President Hugo Chavez danced the joropo outside the Miraflores Palace in Caracas after President Chavez was returned to power following a fourty-eight-hour military coup.**

executed moves that frequently involve stomping their heels or tapping their toes hard on the floor. Although the joropo is performed throughout the country, the dance steps and routine vary slightly from region to region. Six main types of joropo, including Corrido Tuyero and Golpe Aragueño, are popular.

Joropo music is sometimes called *musica llanera* (MOO-see-cah yah-NEH-rah), or music of the plains. Often with either a 3/4 or 6/8 meter, the lively, fast-paced music provides an excellent rhythm to which the stomping moves typical of the dance are performed. Of the many compositions that accompany the dance, *Alma Llanera*, or *Soul of the Plains*, is the most popular. Other compositions include *El Diablo Suelto*, or *The Devil is Free*, and *El Camino Pela'o*, or *The Bare Road*.

Lake Maracaibo

Located in the state of Zulia, Lake Maracaibo has a surface area of about 5,134 square miles (13,300 square km) and is often identified as the largest lake in South America. Lake Maracaibo, however, unlike Lago de Valencia, or Lake Valencia, is not a true lake by definition. Technically, Lake Maracaibo is actually a large, shallow inlet of the Caribbean Sea. A long, narrow strait connects Lake Maracaibo to the Gulf of Venezuela.

Lake Maracaibo is significant and well-loved in Venezuela for a variety of reasons. Returning to the very beginning of Venezuelan history, the country's name — Venezuela — is believed to have been inspired by the Amerindians houses that stood on stilts over the lake's water at the end of the fifteenth century. Italian explorer Amérigo Vespucci, who was employed by the Portuguese, sailed into Lake Maracaibo and sighted the houses on stilts. Vespucci coined the name "Venezuela" to mean "Little Venice." The area's first European settlement, which later became the city of Maracaibo, was established in 1574.

Lake Maracaibo became the subject of much attention in the 1920s, when one of the country's early oil explorations proved successful. The lake, as it turns out, rests on an enormous bed of crude oil. Since then, the city of Maracaibo

Above: **The General Rafael Urdaneta Bridge took five years to build, and construction began in 1958. The bridge measures nearly five and a half miles (9 km).**

Left: **One of the world's longest and most complex bridges, the General Rafael Urdaneta Bridge spans between the states of Zulia and Falcón.**

56

has swiftly expanded and developed into the oil capital of Venezuela, producing up to 70 percent of Venezuela's oil exports. Today, this ultramodern city has a population of approximately 1.3 million and is a major commercial and export center.

While Lake Valencia, Venezuela's only true lake, has been slowly diminishing in size because of intense evaporation and increasing sedimentation, Lake Maracaibo is prevented from a similar fate by a mixture of freshwater and saltwater sources, such as the Caribbean Sea and the Catatumbo River, which both reliably flow into the lake. Extensive commercial and oil-related activies, however, have taken their toll on the environmental condition of the lake. Relentless dredging of the strait connecting Lake Maracaibo to the Gulf of Venezuela has caused the lake's water to become more and more saline. Oil drilling and refining, as well as wastewater produced by the large, nearby urban population, have also led to significant pollution of the lake's water. PDVSA, Venezuela's state-owned oil monopoly, is committed to the process of restoring the lake's natural chemical environment.

Above: **After Lake Maracaibo, Lake Titicaca, which straddles an area between Peru and Bolivia, is South America's second-largest lake.**

Margarita Island

Isla de Margarita, or Margarita Island, measures about 42 miles (67 km) from east to west and about 20 miles (32 km) from north to south. With an area of over 355 square miles (920 square km), the island is especially famous for the stunning beaches that dominate its 103-mile (167-km) coastline. Margarita Island is part of the state of Nueva Esparta, which includes Coche and Cubagua islands to the southeast and south, respectively. Over 350,000 Venezuelans permanently reside on Margarita Island, with about 150,000 living in the city of Porlamar. Although La Asunción is the capital of Nueva Esparta, Porlamar is the larger and more vibrant city. Founded in 1536, Porlamar was first called Puebla de la Mar, meaning "port of the sea," by the Spaniards.

The Guaiqueri Indians were the island's first inhabitants. A friendly and peaceful people, the Guaiqueri were skilled fishers, who were later forced by the Spanish to dive for pearls. Throughout the sixteenth century, shiploads containing thousands of pounds of pearls were sent to Spain from the island.

Below: **The beaches of Margarita Island are world-renowned.**

58

By the seventeenth century, the amount of pearls in the waters around Margarita Island was dramatically depleted. Today, pearls harvested from Margarita Island's surrounding waters are characteristically pink in color, small in size, and unusually shaped. Under Venezuelan laws, pearling is only allowed during certain times of the year to prevent overexploitation.

Visitors to Margarita Island, whether Venezuelan or international, are usually drawn by the island's beaches or shopping. Margarita Island is the country's most favored shopping district because merchandise sold on the island has been tax-free since the mid-1970s. Today, Margarita Island is Venezuela's second-largest tourist attraction, after Caracas. Tourism and fishing form the bedrock of the island's economy.

The Caribbean climate and waters of Margarita Island provide the ideal setting for a wide range of water sports, including swimming, snorkeling, diving, windsurfing, and sailing. The island is also home to many colonial buildings, historical monuments, and museums. For example, the Cathedral of Our Lady of La Asunción was built in 1570, and it is the oldest church in Venezuela.

Above: **Porlamar attracts many Venezuelan and international tourists. Some visitors favor the tax-free shopping that Polamar offers, while others prefer to visit one of the six casinos that operate in the city.**

Oscar D'Leon:
A Salsa Sensation

Oscar D'Leon is one of Venezuela's most famous and well-loved personalities. Known as *El Léon de la Salsa*, which means "The Lion of Salsa," D'Leon's unique voice combined with his immense talent in improvised singing has mesmerized audiences in and out of Venezuela for the last three decades. D'Leon is well known among salsa music lovers for his eclectic style. Salsa music is classified into three main types: New York, Puerto Rican, and South American, which originated from Venezuela, Colombia, and Panama, respectively. D'Leon can creatively blend any of various types of salsa together and even incorporate music from other genres, including jazz, merengue, bolero, paso doble, and ranchera.

D'Leon started his musical career in his thirties, when he played bass guitar in *Dimensión Latina*, a salsa band that became

Left: D'Leon (*far right*) performed at Copacabana, a New York nightclub, in March 2001. D'Leon has also performed in other parts of the United States and various parts of Europe, Asia, and the Caribbean.

hugely popular in the early 1970s. The band's first recording and hit, *Pensando en Tí*, was also his first triumph. By the mid-1970s, D'Leon formed his own band, *La Salsa Mayor*, which played a lot of Cuban music and was equally well received. In 1977, D'Leon recorded his first solo album, *La Salsa Mayor*. In the following year, D'Leon released the best-selling album of his career, *El Más Grande*.

Since his career began over twenty years ago, D'Leon has recorded more than fifty albums, performed internationally at numerous jazz and world music festivals, and worked with other prominent Latin music industry professionals, such as Luís Enriquez, Celia Cruz, José Alberto, and Tito Puente. Puente was mainly responsible for the music in the Hollywood movie *The Mambo Kings* (1992), in which D'Leon gave an acclaimed performance as a guest artist.

D'Leon's achievements have brought him great honors. In New York, for example, D'Leon has performed at Madison Square Garden, Carnegie Hall, and Lincoln Center. In 1988, the New York City Council dedicated a day (March 15) to D'Leon in appreciation of his talents and continued contribution to the city's music scene. In 1996, D'Leon collaborated with famous Cuban musician, Willy Chirino, to produce *Sonero Del Mundo*. The album was nominated for a Grammy award.

Pink Dolphins

Commonly known as the "boto," the pink dolphin (*Inia geoffrensis*) is the world's largest river or freshwater dolphin and can be found in watersheds of the Orinoco river and in the Amazonian region. Fully grown males measure about 9 feet (2.8 m) long and typically weigh between 331 and 441 pounds (150 and 200 kilograms). Adult females are only slightly smaller in size than their male counterparts and give birth to single calves, which usually measure between 28 and 31 inches (70 and 80 centimeters) at birth. Pink dolphin calves are usually born gray and become, in some instances, bright pink as they mature. The average life span of the pink dolphin is unknown but experts believe that it is between fifteen and twenty-five years.

Pink dolphins are mammals, which means that they are warm-blooded and breathe air. Dolphins breathe through blowholes on the tops of their heads. Unlike humans, however, all species of dolphins breathe voluntarily. This means that dolphins have to constantly remind themselves to breathe or they will drown. When dolphins sleep, only one side of their brains rest. The other side remains active to continue the breathing process.

Below: **The pink dolphin is known to eat about fifty species of small fish and shellfish.**

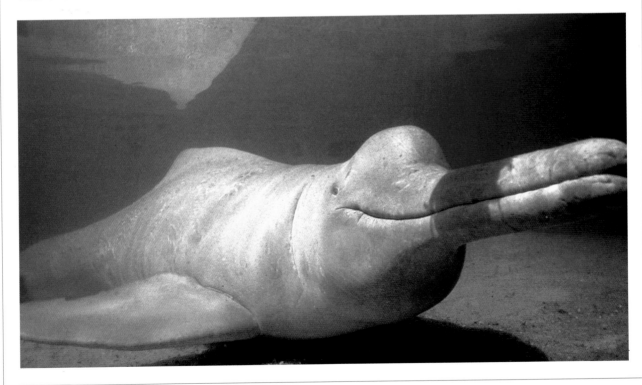

The pink dolphin is unique among all species of dolphins because it has small hairs on its snout. Experts are unsure why the pink dolphin has evolved to have these hairs but have speculated that the hairs are probably meant to increase the dolphin's sense of touch around its snout. Such a function helps the pink dolphin because it characteristically uses its snout to dig through the mud at the bottom of a river in search of the small fish and shellfish on which it relies for food.

Most pink dolphins travel alone or in pairs, but some have been spotted in groups of up to five. Pink dolphins are also quite vocal. They are known to make loud breathing noises when active and produce squawks and clicking noises when underwater.

Unlike the freshwater dolphins of India's Ganges River, Pakistan's Indus River, and China's Yangtze River, the pink dolphin is not an endangered species. Pink dolphins living in the Orinoco River and its tributaries are mainly threatened by hydropower plants, oil pollution, and mercury pollution caused by gold mining, but Venezuelan authorities have been careful to ensure that the dolphins continue to thrive in large numbers.

Above: **The pink dolphin has been described as friendly, extremely curious, and as playful as a child.**

Political Unrest in 2002

In 2000, President Hugo Chavez was reelected president for the next six years. In 2001, Chavez implemented a set of radical reform policies that led the Venezuelan economy to a dramatic crash by February 2002. Venezuela's currency, the bolivar, had fallen by 25 percent against the U.S. dollar, PDVSA's profit for 2001 had dropped over 40 percent from that of 2000, and nineteen high-level excutives of PDVSA had been fired and replaced with yes-men from the Chavez administration.

On April 9, 2002, trade unions and business executives came together to declare a general strike in response to Chavez's questionable handling of PDVSA. On April 11, a group of gunmen fired shots into the 150,000-strong crowd demonstrating outside Miraflores Palace, the home of President Chavez. The military blamed Chavez for the gunmen's ruthless actions and removed him from office the next day. Pedro Carmona, a key opposition leader, replaced Chavez as president. Carmona took the opportunity to immediately dismiss many government officials and dissolve the country's constitution. On April 12, thousands of pro-Chavez Venezuelans marched in the streets of Caracas demanding his reinstatement. Mounting violence and

CONTROVERSIAL CHAVEZ

In 2000, Chavez became the first president to visit Iraq since the Persian Gulf War in 1991. Chavez acted despite strong opposition from the United States, the largest buyer of Venezuelan exports. Chavez is also a self-confessed admirer of Fidel Castro's Cuba.

Left and *above:* On November 18, 2002, Guardia Nacional, or National Guard, soldiers fired tear gas into demonstrating crowds in Caracas. The crowd was protesting the absorbtion of the Caracas police force by the military, which is headed by President Chavez. On December 18, 2002, the Supreme Court ordered the Chavez government to return control of the police force to Alfredo Pena, the mayor of Caracas.

pressure led Carmona's government to collapse, and Chavez was returned to office on April 14. Venezuela's constitution was also quickly restored. More than twenty lives were lost in the forty-eight-hour coup.

By October 2002, even working-class Venezuelans, who had previously been Chavez's strongest supporters, were enraged by the ailing economy and a string of failed promises. They joined the country's upper and middle classes in calling for either Chavez's resignation or early elections. While the Venezuelan constitution does not provide for early elections, it does allow opposition leaders to pursue a referendum. In Venezuela, the results of a referendum are not binding, but opposition leaders had hoped that negative results in the voting would embarrass Chavez to the point where he would voluntarily resign.

In late November 2002, anti-Chavez oil workers and executives began a prolonged general strike in an attempt to pressure Chavez into calling for early elections. By mid-December, the country's oil production had been brought to a total standstill and a host of export contracts had been left unmet. Clashes between pro- and anti-Chavez forces grew increasingly violent, continued into 2003, and severely hurt the economy.

Above: **Anti-Chavez Venezuelans block a freeway in Caracas during one of many demonstrations in 2002.**

REFERENDUM BLOCKED

The Venezuelan constitution states that the National Electoral Council has to gather a minimum of 1.2 million signatures in support of a common cause before a referendum can be pursued. On November 4, 2002, the electoral council submitted 2 million signatures and demanded that Chavez arrange a referendum by December or risk a nationwide strike. In late November, the Venezuelan Supreme Court stopped the referendum proceedings based on a legal technicality.

Saving Venezuela: Environmental Projects

Established in 1977, Venezuela's Ministry of Environment and Renewable Natural Resources was one of the first government-run environmental protection agencies in Latin America. The ministry is committed to addressing environmental issues, such as deforestation, urban pollution, and rural soil degradation. Apart from the ministry, many large corporations are also doing their part to maintain a cleaner environment. Formed in 1987, Provita is a Caracas-based conservation group dedicated to educating and helping corporations develop projects that allow industrial advancement without compromising environmental conservation and the protection of endangered animals.

Among the many programs that Provita has initiated over the years are Proyecto Integrado de Conservación y Desarrollo Costa de Barlovento (Integrated Conservation and Development Project Costa Barlovento) and Programa Amazonas (Amazonas

ALTERNATIVE ENERGY SOURCES

Although Venezuela is one of the world's largest producers of oil, the country utilizes mostly hydroelectric power. Venezuela has no nuclear power plants.

Below: Venezuela's Caribbean coast is home to a rich but fragile ecosystem.

Left: The lush, tropical Amazonian rain forests in Guayana and Amazonas are among the last of their kind in the world.

Program). PDVSA is the sole sponsor of the former project, which began in 1999 and is aimed at promoting conservation-minded practices along Venezuela's Caribbean coast, where the preservation of endangered marine turtles is a primary concern. Provita, the Ministry of Environment and Renewable Natural Resources, and various business and community organizations also participated in the project. The state of Miranda was the first in the country to benefit from this program, which was scheduled to have expanded to other coastal cities at the beginning of 2002.

Programa Amazonas, also initiated in 1999, is solely sponsored by the Netherlands Organisation for International Development Cooperation (NOVIB). The program seeks to improve the lives of indigenous peoples inhabiting the country's Amazonian rain forests by supplementing their dwindling food sources with alternative food and cash crops and without taking too much away from their traditional practices. If proven sustainable, the program will be applied to indigenous peoples inhabiting other lowland forests in Venezuela.

ECOTOURISM

Ecotourism is tourism that privileges and respects the beauty and spectacle of a country's natural environment. Ecotourism allows the Venezuelan government to protect the country's natural environment, educate the public, and generate income from tourist dollars all at once.

The Venezuelan government protects over 40 percent of the country's land, which includes forty-two national parks and the sites of twenty-one national monuments. Over twenty-five different ecosystems are found within the country.

Simón Bolívar: Founding Father

On July 24, 1783, Simón Bolívar was born to wealthy Creole parents, both of whom died by the time he was nine years old. Young Bolívar was placed in the care of his uncle, Carlos Palacios, who sent him to Spain to pursue higher education when he turned sixteen. Under a group of esteemed tutors, Bolívar was schooled in the works of great thinkers, such as John Locke, Thomas Hobbes, François Voltaire, and Jean Jacques Rousseau. In 1802, Bolívar married Maria Teresa Rodríguez del Toro y Alaysa, the daughter of a Spanish nobleman, and returned to Caracas with his new bride. She died of yellow fever less than one year later, and Bolívar swore he would never marry again.

Today, Bolívar is widely remembered as the founding father of Venezuela, as well as of several neighboring South American countries, because of his lifetime of remarkable and relentless

Below: **A group of schoolchildren visit Simón Bolívar's birthplace in order to learn more about the great leader's past.**

Left: Simón Bolívar, whose full name was Simón José Antonio de la Santísmia Trinidad Bolívar, is widely honored in South America as *El Libertador*, which means "the Liberator." Some people have called him the "George Washington of South America."

resistance efforts in the region against the Spanish crown. His vision was to liberate and unite the whole of South America in Gran Colombia, the union of present-day Venezuela, Colombia, Panama, and Ecuador founded by Bolívar in 1819.

In Venezuela, Bolívar and his army secured a landmark victory against the Spanish at the Battle of Carabobo in 1821. By 1823, the Battle of Puerto Cabello was won under the leadership of General José Antonio Paéz, and the last of the Spanish troops were driven out. In the two years that followed, Bolívar headed further south to liberate first Peru and then Bolivia. While Bolívar was away, however, internal disputes in Gran Colombia escalated and the union began to divide. Venezuela eventually broke free in 1829 and Ecuador in 1830. In 1830, Venezuela adopted a new constitution that declared itself an independent country, and General José Antonio Paéz became Venezuela's first president.

Bolívar, unfortunately, died in Colombia on December 17, 1830, a penniless and disillusioned man.

BOLÍVAR'S PLACE OF REST

The Panteon Nacional in Caracas is a large mausoleum, where the remains of Simón Bolívar and other prominent historical figures from Venezuela's past are laid to rest. The exterior of the Panteon Nacional is unremarkable, but the interior is opulent. Although open to the public, the mausoleum is guarded twenty-four hours a day, and the guards have the right to turn away visitors that are inappropriately dressed or remove those not behaving respectfully while inside the site.

Valencia: Old City, New City

Located about 90 miles (145 km) southwest of Caracas, Valencia is the capital city of the state of Carabobo and is famous as the country's main manufacturing center. In the last decade of the twentieth century, Valencia experienced rapid growth and development, which led the city to absorb the neighboring towns of Naguanagua, Los Guayos, Central Tacarigua, Tocuyito, and Carabobo. In 2001, Valencia had an estimated population of 1.8 million people.

Founded in 1555, Valencia was invaded, destroyed, and rebuilt on several occasions during the city's early history. Valencia also served twice as the capital of Venezuela, first and briefly in 1812 and again in 1830, when Venezuela broke away from Gran Colombia to become an independent nation. In 1812, Valencia was utterly destroyed by an earthquake. Of all the historical highlights in Valencia's colorful history, however, the most significant would have to be the Batalla de Carabobo, or Battle of Carabobo, which was fought in 1821. The battle was the first in a series of events that ultimately secured Venezuela's independence from Spain. Today, a national monument, called Parque Campo de Carabobo, or the Field of Carabobo Park, marks the site where the battle was fought.

Today, Valencia is a bustling industrial city. Its many factories mainly produce petrochemicals, pharmeceuticals, processed food, and textiles. Valencia is also known for the massive car assembly plant that Ford established in 1962. Because Valencia is the nearest major city to the Llanos, where herds of cattle are reared and cash crops such as cotton and sugarcane, are grown, the city is also where much of the country's agricultural produce is sold. Business in Valencia use the seaport of Puerto Cabello to handle the demands of international trade.

Valencia is also home to the respected Universidad de Carabobo, which was founded in 1892. La Plaza Monumental de Valencia, located southeast of the city, is one of the world's largest bullfighting rings and the largest in South America. The plaza has a maximum seating capacity of 27,000 people.

Above: **Many original colonial buildings in the city of Valencia have been preserved.**

Opposite: **In the heart of Valencia are numerous historical and cultural sites, including La Plaza Bolívar, which was built in honor of Venezuelan hero and liberator, Simon Bolivar, and La Casa Páez, which was the home of Venezuela's first president, General José Antonio Páez. La Catedral de Valencia is one of Valencia's many beautiful, old churches.**

The Women of Venezuela

In Venezuela, as is the case in other Latin American countries, the older or more traditional members of society may expect men to demonstrate machismo. Traits of machismo include strength, aggressiveness, a domineering attitude toward women, and virility that sometimes excuses infidelity. Although the Equal Opportunities Act was passed in 1993, gender discrimination in Venezuela has not vanished. Sexual harassment, whether physical or verbal, is common for working Venezuelan women, who generally earn between 30 and 40 percent less than the country's men. Many Venezuelan women also suffer domestic violence. In 1999, the Law on Violence Against Women and Family was passed.

The most disadvantaged group of women in Venezuela is single mothers. In 1999, nearly half of Venezuelan single mothers were living in poverty, and even extreme poverty, while trying to raise their children and make ends meet. In a 2002 report prepared by the Canadian International Development Agency

AN ARCHAIC LAW

Under current Venezuelan law, a man who rapes a woman he knows can avoid punishment if he marries her before he is sentenced in court.

Increasingly, however, new laws and government agencies such as the Direccion General Sectorial para la Mujer (Sectorial General Directorate for Women) and the Instituto Nacional de la Mujer (National Women's Institute) are being established to help and protect the modern Venezuelan woman.

(CIDA) under the Industrial Cooperation Program (ICP), only 63 percent of female heads of households were part of the Venezuelan workforce as opposed to 91 percent of male heads of households. The report also said that children of female-headed households, including the children of single mothers, tended to become pregnant or marry early and not finish their education, thus perpetuating the cycle of poverty.

Venezuelan women, however, have come a long way in the last two decades of the twentieth century, with women consistently accounting for about half of all students attending Venezuelan universities. In 1999, 5 percent more female than male teenagers living in urban Venezuela were attending school. Between 1995 and 2001, the number of women in the Venezuelan parliament increased from 6 to 10 percent. More Venezuelan women are also assuming administrative and managerial positions, with the percentage rising from thirteen in the mid-1980s to twenty-three in the mid-1990s. Nevertheless, Venezuelan women in general still earn between one-quarter to one-third less than their male counterparts.

Above: Previously, women in Venezuela tended to work in the service industries. Today, Venezuelan women are venturing into previously male-dominated professions, such as finance, law enforcement, and real estate.

Opposite: A group of female students play a game of soccer at the Universidad Central de Venzuela.

RELATIONS WITH NORTH AMERICA

Venezuela's relations with North America date back to the 1800s, when influential leaders, such as General Francisco de Miranda and Simón Bolívar, were inspired by the North American liberation movement. In the second half of the 1900s, two major events in Venezuelan history facilitated the country's relations with North America. First, Venezuela was among the first Latin American countries to embrace democracy. Second, Venezuela discovered and developed its vast oil resources. Relations between the country and the United States became troubled in 2002. In April 2002, the Chavez government was overthrown by a

Opposite: **The people of Venezuela have long been exposed to the products made by large U.S. companies.**

military coup for two days. During this time, the U.S. government openly approved of the new administration, which had members who were known to have met frequently with U.S. government officials before the coup. Many Venezuelans were angered by U.S. actions, regarding them as a violation of the Inter-American Democratic Charter and the Betancourt Doctrine, both of which state that governments created by coups or other undemocratic means should not be recognized as legitimate governments. When Chavez was returned to power two days later, some hard feelings remained between the Venezuelan and U.S. governments.

Above: **Employed to work on a joint venture between Venezuela and the United States, these two Venezuelans work at an oil field near Lake Maracaibo.**

Ties with the United States

Venezuela and the United States shared a stable relationship for much of the 1900s. The relationship, however, has encompassed little more than bilateral trade concerns and issues. According to 2002 figures from the U.S. Department of State, the United States imported Venezuelan products totaling U.S. $15.8 billion in 2001. Venezuela sells more than half of the country's oil exports to the United States, where it is a top supplier of foreign oil to the United States. Venezuela is also one of the top export markets for the United States in Latin America. In 2001, Venezuela imported U.S. goods amounting to U.S. $5.8 billion.

In fact, the United States viewed trade relations between the two nations as so vital that former U.S. president Bill Clinton paid Venezuela an official visit in October 1997. President Clinton's visit was significant because PDVSA, Venezuela's state-owned oil monopoly, had just opened its petroleum sector to foreign investment a year earlier. PDVSA's move created overnight an abundance of lucrative opportunities for U.S. companies. During his visit, President Clinton specifically promoted a program called

Left: **Former presidents Rafael Caldera Rodriguez (*left*) and Bill Clinton (*right*) inspect the Venezuelan guard of honor on October 13, 1997, when Clinton paid an official visit.**

"Partnership for the Twenty-first Century," which emphasized greater cooperation between the two nations in their pursuit of common goals, such as developing mutually beneficial energy solutions, trade and investment policies, antidrug strategies, and environmental protection plans.

Relations between Venezuela and the United States, however, have soured since President Hugo Chavez came to power in 1998. The governments of both countries have since failed to see eye to eye on several international issues, and Chavez's outspoken ways have further offended many U.S. leaders and officials. Chavez, for example, heavily criticized U.S. actions in Afghanistan following the terrorist attacks on New York's World Trade Center on September 11, 2001. He has been quoted as saying that the large number of civilian deaths caused by aggressive U.S. military actions in Afghanistan is, in effect, no different from the injustices inflicted on innocent U.S. civilians by terrorists in their attacks on the World Trade Center.

Above: U.S. soldiers in Caracas load a military helicopter with food supplies headed for the state of Vargas. On December 15, 1999, Venezuela suffered one of the world's worst natural disasters in recent times. Rainstorms and rising floodwaters led to a series of mud slides that devastated parts of eleven states, including the city of Caracas. Between 10,000 and 20,000 lives were lost. The United States sent 107 military personnel, ten helicopters, and five transport airplanes to Venezuela to provide disaster relief.

Ties with Canada

Relations between Canada and Venezuela have always been friendly. Similar to U.S.-Venezuelan relations, a great deal of Canada's dealings with Venezuela were, and still are, based on trade. In 1997, the two countries signed the Foreign Investment Protection Agreement, and in 1999, they entered into the Canada-Andean Community Trade and Investment Cooperation Agreement (TICA).

Today, Venezuela is Canada's second-largest South American trade partner, after Brazil. In 2001, trade between the two countries totaled U.S. $2.14 billion, and Canadian investments in Venezuela amounted to about U.S. $210 million. In the past, Canadian investors have tended to favor Venezuela's energy, mining, telecommunications, and banking sectors. Entering the twenty-first century, Canadian investors and exporters are looking to diversify their interests and have been investigating Venezuela's agricultural, food, forestry, and environmental sectors for potential trade opportunities.

In 2001, Canada exported U.S. $792 million worth of goods to Venezuela and, in turn, imported U.S. $1.35 billion of Venezuelan goods. Canadian exports to Venezuela included cars, car parts and accessories, telecommunication and oil field

Left: On April 22, 2001, Canadian prime minister Jean Chretien (*left*) and Venezuelan president Hugo Chavez (*right*) shake hands after signing an agreement at the third Summit of the Americas, held in Quebec. The agreement will help to create the world's largest Free Trade Zone by 2005.

Left: U.S. president George W. Bush (*center*) meets with the leaders of the Andean nations, including Venezuelan president Hugo Chavez (*far left*), Peruvian prime minister Javier Perez de Cuellar (*second from left*), Panamanian president Mireya Elisa Moscoso (*third from right*), Colombian president Andres Pastrana (*second from right*), and Ecuadorian president Gustavo Noboa Bejarano (*far right*), on April 20, 2001 to discuss free trade issues The meeting marked the beginning of the 2001 Summit of Americas.

equipment, wood pulp, computers, and agricultural produce, such as wheat, lentils, beans, and potatoes. Venezuela, on the other hand, exported mainly petroleum, petrochemicals, iron, steel, bitumen, rubber, and plastic to Canada.

In 2001, over 92 percent of Canadian agricultural exports to Venezuela were provided by Saskatchewan, Manitoba, and Alberta combined. Although Venezuela's agricultural sector is generally underdeveloped, the country's growers still managed to export a modest amount of agricultural goods, valued at U.S. $1.9 million, to Canada in 2001. Venezuela's agricultural exports to Canada consisted mainly of cashews and sesame seeds.

Trade relations between Venezuela and Canada also extend to the oil industry. In early 2002, Veba Oil and Gas (VOG), a German, government-related oil conglomerate, sold its international operations, which included Veba Oel de Venezuela (VOV), to Petro-Canada. VOV and PDVSA have maintained a close working relationship since 1978. Petro-Canada's recent acquisition makes it the largest integrated oil and gas company in Canada and a significant force in the world market.

Canada and Venezuela share diplomatic concerns. Both countries are part of the United Nations Friends of Haiti group and have pledged support for each other under the Organization of American States (OAS). Venezuela also receives support from the Canadian International Development Agency (CIDA).

North Americans in Venezuela

According to figures from the U.S. State Department, about 23,000 U.S. citizens were living in Venezuela in 1999. The deparment also estimated that about 12,000 Americans visit Venezuela each year. Ecotourism is what attracts most American tourists to Venezuela, and popular destinations include the country's Caribbean islands, Amazonian rain forests, and Guiana Highlands. Americans who live in Venezuela on a more permanent basis include government representatives, businesspeople, aid workers, and missionaries.

In 1999, about 500 U.S. companies had offices in Venezuela. Apart from oil-industry heavyweights, such as ExxonMobil and ChevronTexaco, and fast-food retailers, such as McDonalds and Burger King, Ford Motor de Venezuela, S. A. is probably the next most prominent U.S. business in Venezuela. The Venezuelan plant of the Ford Motor Company, established in 1962, is located in the industrial area of the city of Valencia and covers about 4,480,343 square feet (416,234 square m). The plant is so large that the street it is on is called the Avenida Henry Ford. The Ford company has about 1,500 employees, who work in two shifts. Every day, the plant produces 300 vehicles. Although the factory's output

Below: **As of July 2002, Venezuela had twenty Burger King fast-food outlets. The country's first Burger King opened in 1980.**

Left: **Venezuelan president Hugo Chavez (*left*) and U.S. ambassador Charles Shapiro (*right*) met for diplomatic talks on August 3, 2002 at the Miraflores Palace in Caracas.**

consists mostly of the Festiva and the Fiesta models, the plant also assembes commercial vehicles and the Explorer model, which is a four-wheel-drive sport utility vehicle.

Both the United States and Canada have embassies in Venezuela. Charles Shapiro is the U.S. ambassador to Venezuela, while Allan Culham is the Canadian ambassador. Both ambassadors assumed their positions in 2002. The two nations are also represented in Venezuela by trade-facilitating institutions, such as the Venezuelan-American Chamber of Commerce (VACC) and the Canadian-Venezuelan Chamber of Commerce (CVCC). The VACC was founded in 1950 and the CVCC in 1987.

Apart from tourism and private-sector industry, Canadian presence in Venezuela is also felt indirectly through various aid programs and agencies, such as the United Nations Children's Fund (UNICEF), the World Bank, and the Inter-American Development Bank. The Canadian International Development Agency (CIDA) does not have a bilateral program with Venezuela, but CIDA supports a number of programs that provide Venezuela with assistance. The Canadian Partnership Branch, for example, is a program designed to link Canadian organizations with developing countries in the hope that the partnership will lead to sustainable development and reduced poverty for the developing nation.

Venezuelans in North America

Figures from the U.S. Census Bureau suggest that approximately 31 million Latin Americans live in the United States. Latin Americans form the largest immigrant group in the United States and about 11.2 percent of the country's population. Venezuelans, however, do not figure prominently among the Latin American immigrants, who mostly originate from Mexico, the Dominican Republic, Cuba, and Jamaica.

In Canada, new Venezuelan immigrants can choose to enter the country's Host Program, which ensures that they are given a warm welcome upon arrival in Canada, as well as a helping hand in building a new home and life. One of the first things host families do is to show the newcomers where to do their grocery shopping and banking or where to find major services.

Canada also encourages cross-cultural interaction among university professors. The country welcomes teaching staff from Venezuelan universities under the Canadian Studies Faculty Enrichment Award Program. This program educates Venezuelan professors about Canada, so that they can return to their homeland and develop university courses in Canadian studies.

Venezuela is also represented by two embassies in North America — one in the United States and one in Canada. In the United States, the Embassy of the Republic of Venezuela is located in Washington, D.C. In Canada, the Venezuelan embassy is located in Ottawa.

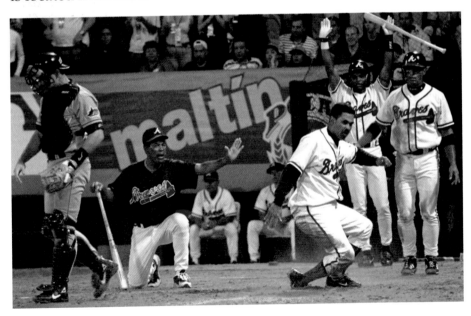

Left: **Venezuelan Ozzie Guillen (***third from right***) recovers from a slide during a baseball game played in Caracas on March 18, 2000. Guillen was playing for the Atlanta Braves, who were playing against the Tampa Bay Devil Rays.**

Famous Venezuelans

Famous Venezuelans in North America include baseball player Andres Galarraga (1961–) and basketball player Carl Herrera (1966–). A talented first baseman, Galarraga played for the Montreal Expos in 2002 and signed with the San Francisco Giants for 2003. Herrera, on the other hand, is the only Latin American in the world to have won the National Basketball Association (NBA) championships. He was first drafted at NBA level in 1990, when he played for the Houston Rockets. Herrera has also played for the San Antonio Spurs and the Denver Nuggets.

Entertainer Mariah Carey has some Venezuelan heritage. Born in 1970 to a half-black, half-Venezuelan father, Alfred Roy Carey, and an Irish mother, Patricia Hickey, Carey first became famous in 1990, when her self-titled, debut album was released. The album included a string of hits, such as "Vision of Love," "Love Takes Time," "Someday," and "I Don't Wanna Cry." Carey released her latest album, *Charmbracelet*, in 2002.

Above: As of 2000, more than 125 million copies of Carey's albums had been sold worldwide. Carey remains the only female artist to have had fifteen number-one songs on the U.S. Hot 100 charts.

Above: **Venezuelan women from all walks of life came together on November 28, 2002 to launch a peaceful protest against President Hugo Chavez in Caracas.**

Women's Campaign International

In October 1999, the U.S. embassy in Venezuela invited the United States-based organization Women's Campaign International to Venezuela to conduct two training sessions — one in Caracas and one in Maracaibo. Each training session lasted for two days, and their immediate objectives included an exchange of ideas between the women of both countries, educating budding Venezuelan women politicians on how to launch successful political campaigns, and creating a greater awareness of women's issues in the Venezuelan media. The larger, more long-term objective of the project was to have the women of both countries build friendships and later cooperate in their joint attempt to promote and achieve lasting peace and democracy in Venezuela.

Both training sessions conducted by Women's Campaign International were sponsored by the United States Information Agency (USIA). Founded in 1953, the USIA is an independent agency that promotes U.S. foreign policy and national interests in other countries by encouraging cultural exchanges and putting together educational, broadcasting, and information programs.

Women's Campaign International also received strong support from the U.S. embassy in Venezuela, the Women's Council of Venezuela (CONOMU), and the Governor's Office of the state of Zulia. The training sessions were so successful that Women's Campaign International returned to Venezuela in June 2000.

Global Women's Strike

In July 2002, Venezuela's Instituto Nacional de la Mujer, or National Women's Institute, invited members of Global Women's Strike, an international nongovernmental organization (NGO) with several U.S. branches, to Venezuela. The purpose of their visit was to help create an international support network that acts to hinder, if not prevent, future military coups and potential assasinations from unfolding in Venezuela and elsewhere in the world. Calls for such a network intensified after 2002, when President Chavez was forcibly removed from power. Although the U.S. government denied it had any part in the dramatic upheaval, some NGOs, such as Global Women's Strike, are of the opinion it was a military coup supported by the U.S. government. By praising the transitional government headed by Pedro Carmona, the interim president, who dissolved the constitution and dismissed a series of government officials, the U.S. government had temporarily positioned itself in unfavorable light.

Above: **Thousands of Venezuelan women marched in Caracas streets on International Women's Day (March 8) in 2002. The women, however, were divided; one camp was for and one against President Chavez. Women on both sides sought to make their voices heard without violence.**

Left: **These Venezuelan women are marching in a demonstration and protesting against President Chavez in the streets of Caracas on October 3, 2002.**

VENEZUELA

ATLANTIC OCEAN

C A R I B B E A N   S E A

Islas Los Roques

Península de Paraguaná

Gulf of Venezuela

TRINIDAD AND TOBAGO

Margarita Island
Cubagua Island
Coche Island

Paria Peninsula

19 • La Asunción
• Porlamar

• Maracaibo

20

SIERRA DE PERIJÁ

Lago de Maracaibo

5

11

6

• Barquisimeto

Morón •
Valencia •

Puerto Cabello •

12

14

15 • Cumaná
• Barcelona

• Caripito
• Caripe

CARACAS
• Petare

16

Puerto La Cruz •

COASTAL CORDILLERA

21

4

• Jajo • Trujillo

C O R D I L L E R A

3

7

• San Carlos

10

Lago de Valencia

• Maracay

13

Catatumbo

• Mérida
• Colón

SIERRA DE MÉRIDA

• Barinas
Pico Bolívar (16,428ft.)

2

8

L L A N O S

17

18

Orinoco Delta

22

• Ciudad Guayana

• Ciudad Bolívar

9

Orinoco

23

GUYANA

Andes Mountains

C O L O M B I A

G U I A N A HIGHLANDS

Churún Merú (3,212 ft.)

La Gran Sabana

Caroní

24

SIERRA PARIMA

Casiquiare

Orinoco

B R A Z I L

———	Country Boundary
———	State Boundary
■	Capital
●	City
～～	River

N

Above: Venezuela's Amazonian rain forests are rich in bird life.

Andes Mountains A3
Atlantic Ocean D1

Barcelona C2
Barinas A2–A3
Barquisimeto B2
Brazil B5–D3

Caracas B2
Caribbean Sea A1–C1
Caripe C2
Caripito C2
Caroní River D3–D4
Casiquiare River A4–C4
Catatumbo River A2–A3
Churún Merú D3
Ciudad Bolivar C3
Ciudad Guayana D3
Coastal Cordillera
    B2–D2
Coche Island C2
Colombia A1–B5
Colón A3
Cordillera (region)
    A2–A3
Cubagua Island C2
Cumaná C2

Guiana Highlands
    (region) C3–D4

Gulf of Venezuela A2
Guyana D3–D4

Islas Los Roques
    B1–B2

Jajo A2

La Asunción C2
La Gran Sabana D3–D4
Lago de Maracaibo A2
Lago de Valencia B2
Llanos (region) A3–C3

Maracaibo A2
Maracay B2
Margarita Island C2
Mérida A3
Morón B2

Orinoco Delta D2–D3
Orinoco River B3–D2
Orinoco River
    (odd branch) B3–C4

Paria Peninsula D2
Peninsula de Paraguaná
    A1–B2
Petare B2–C2
Pico Bolívar A3

Porlamar C2
Puerto Cabello B2
Puerto La Cruz C2

San Carlos B2
Sierra de Mérida A3–B2
Sierra de Períja A2–A3
Sierra Parima C4

Trinidad and Tobago D2
Trujillo A2

Valencia B2

States

1 Zulia

2 Táchira

3 Mérida

4 Trujillo

5 Falcón

6 Lara

7 Portuguesa

8 Barinas

9 Apure

10 Cojedes

11 Yaracuy

12 Carabobo

13 Aragua

14 Distrito Federal

15 Vargas

16 Miranda

17 Guárico

18 Anzoátegui

19 Nueva Esparta

20 Sucre

21 Monagas

22 Delta Amacuro

23 Bolívar

24 Amazonas

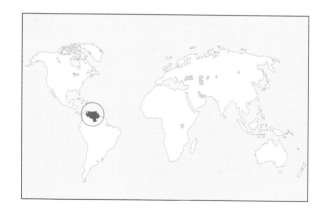

VENEZUELA

A B C D

1

2

3

4

5

How Is Your Geography?

Learning to identify the main geographical areas and points of a country can be challenging. Although it may seem difficult at first to memorize the locations and spellings of major cities or the names of mountain ranges, rivers, deserts, lakes, and other prominent physical features, the end result of this effort can be very rewarding. Places you previously did not know existed will suddenly come to life when referred to in world news, whether in newspapers, television reports, other books and reference sources, or on the Internet. This knowledge will make you feel a bit closer to the rest of the world, with its fascinating variety of cultures and physical geography.

This map can be duplicated for use in a classroom. (PLEASE DO NOT WRITE IN THIS BOOK!) Students can then fill in any requested information on their individual map copies. The student can also make a copy of the map and use it as a study tool to practice identifying place names and geographical features on his or her own.

Above: **A young girl from Porlamar sits by a few pieces of locally made pottery.**

Venezuela at a Glance

Official Name The Bolivarian Republic of Venezuela

Capital Caracas

Official Language Spanish

Population 23.9 million (July 2001 estimate)

Land Area 352,015 square miles 912,050 (square kilometers)

Highest Point Pico Bolivar 16,428 feet (5,007 meters)

Longest River Rio Orinoco 1,590 miles (2,560 km)

Largest Lake Lago de Maracaibo

Main Religion Roman Catholicism

Ethnic Groups Mestizos (67 percent), Europeans (21 percent), African (10 percent), Amerindian (2 percent)

Administrative regions Amazonas, Anzoátegui, Apure, Aragua, Barinas, Bolívar, Carabobo, Cojedes, Delta, Dependencia Federal, Distrito Federal, Falcón, Guárico, Lara, Mérida, Miranda, Monagas, Nueva Esparta, Portuguesa, Sucre, Táchira, Trujillo, Yaracuy, Vargas, Zulia.

Holidays Battle of Carabobo (June 24)

Independence Day (July 5)

Simón Bolívar's Birthday (July 24)

Día de la Raza (October 12)

Exports Petroleum, petrochemicals, bauxite, metalworks, agricultural produce, consumer goods

Imports Machinery, transportation equipment, construction materials

Major Trade Partners United States, Columbia, Brazil, Canada, Japan, Germany, Italy, France,

Currency Bolivar (VEB 1,600.00 = U.S. $1 as of 2003)

Opposite: **A man holds a piranha caught in a river that flows through the Amazonian rain forest.**

Glossary

Spanish Vocabulary

abuelitos (ah-bway-LEE-tohs): grandparents.

Andinos (ahn-DEE-nohs): Andean people whose towns and villages in and near the Andes mountains typically date back to Spanish colonial times.

arepa (ah-REH-pah): a piece of fried dough made from cornflour, salt, and water.

bolas criollas (BOH-lahs cree-OH-yahs): lawn bowling.

chicha de arroz (CHEE-chah deh ah-ROHS): a sweet dessert made from rice starch, milk, vanilla, and sugar.

cuatro (coo-AH-troh): a small, four-stringed guitar.

dependencia federal (deh-penn-DEHN-see-ah feh-deh-RAHL): federal dependency.

distrito federal (dees-TREE-toh feh-deh-RAHL): federal district.

estados (ehs-TAH-dohs): states.

gente cualquiera (HEN-teh coo-ahl-kee-EH-rah): literally "common people;" members of society's lower class.

gente decente (HEN-teh deh-SEHN-teh): literally "decent people;" members of society's upper class.

Guayanés (goo-ah-yah-NEHS): people who reside in the Amazonian forests.

hallaca (ah-YAH-kah): a Venezuelan dish made from cornmeal, beef, pork, chicken, green peppers, tomatoes, onions, garlic, olives, rasins, and various herbs and spices.

llaneros (yah-NEH-rohs): cowboys of the Llanos region in central Venezuela.

madrina (mah-DREE-nah): godmother.

merengada (meh-rehn-GAH-dah): milkshakes flavored with the juices of fresh fruits.

musica llanera (MOO-see-cah yah-NEH-rah): music of the plains.

Pabellón Criollo (pah-beh-YOHN cree-OH-yoh): a stew made from shredded beef and typically eaten with rice, black beans, and fried plantains.

padrino (pah-DREE-noh): godfather.

papelon con limon (pah-peh-LOHN kohn lee-MOHN): a kind of lemonade that is sweetened with raw sugar instead of refined sugar.

perico (peh-REE-koh): scrambled eggs tossed with tomatoes and onions.

ranchos (RAHN-chohs): shantytowns.

English Vocabulary

acquainted: having been brought into social contact; familiar.

altitudinal: relating to height or the distance upward.

animistic: believing that natural objects, natural phenomena, and the universe itself possess souls.

austerity: strict economy, nonmaterialism, and self-denial.

bilateral: affecting two nations or parties.

cacao: the dried seeds of a South American tree that are used in making cocoa and chocolate.

cannibalistic: related to the practice of human being eating human flesh.

commonplace: ordinary; everyday.

compromising: settling for less than the best that could be achieved.

contaminated: to make polluted by mixing with toxic or unclean substances.

cosmopolitan: made up of people or elements from many parts of the world; having international sophistication.

degradation: the process of lowering in quality, rank, or status.

deforestation: the large-scale clearing of trees or forests.

dredging: removing sand or silt from the bottom of a river or other body of water.

epidemic: where a disease has spread rapidly throughout a given area.

esteemed: regarded with respect or admiration.

hydroelectric power: electricity generated from waterpower.

infidelity: marital unfaithfulness; adultery.

influential: having or exerting influence.

initiated: begun or originated.

lichens: complex plants made up of a fungus and an alga growing together.

lucrative: profitable; moneymaking.

mausoleum: a stone building containing above-ground tombs.

meandering: proceeding by a winding or indirect course.

petrochemicals: chemicals derived from petroleum or natural gas.

pharmaceuticals: medicinal drugs.

picturesque: visually charming or quaint, as if resembling a painting.

precarious: uncertain or unsteady and, thus, dangerous.

prosperity: a successful, flourishing, or thriving condition, especially in economic matters.

quinessential: having the essence of a thing in its purest form.

referendum: a vote on a matter that a country's legislative body presents to the voting public for their approval or refusal.

relentless: showing no decrease in severity, strength, or intensity.

Romanticism: the movement in literature and art, usually contrasted with Classicism, that emphasizes imagination and emotion.

ruthlessness: the state of being merciless, cruel, and without pity or compassion.

saline: consisting of or containing salt.

Spanish Inquisition: the court that existed between the late fifteenth and mid-nineteenth centuries and persecuted non-Roman Catholic residents of Spain and many of its colonies.

stagnant: not flowing and stale.

subtropical: relating to regions bordering tropical zones.

sustainable: possible to uphold or keep going without permanent damage or depletion of resources.

tributaries: streams that flow to larger streams or rivers.

tumultuous: full of disorder and agitation.

undulating: having a wavy form or rising-and-falling surface.

venomous: having a gland or glands that secrete a poison; able to inflict a poisonous bite or sting.

vigor: active strength or energy; intensity; effective force.

virility: the quality of being manly in character and spirit.

More Books to Read

Amazon: A Young Reader's Look at the Last Frontier. Peter Lourie (Boyd Mills Press)

The Birds of Venezuela. Steven L. Hilty (Princeton University Press)

Faces of the Rainforest: The Yanomami. Valdir Cruz (Powerhouse Books)

Latin American Arts and Cultures. Dorothy Chaplik (Davis)

The Orinoco River. Watts Library: World of Water series. Carol B. Rawlins (Franklin Watts)

Simon Bolivar: South American Liberator. Hispanic Biographies series. David Goodnough (Enslow Publishers)

Venezuela. Cultures of the World series. Jane Kohen Winter and Kitt Baguley (Benchmark Books)

Venezuela. Discovering South America series. Charles J. Shields (Lerner Publications)

Venezuela in Pictures. Visual Geography series. Lincoln A. Boehm (Mason Crest)

The Yanomami of South America. Raya Tahan (Lerner)

Videos

Land of the Anaconda. (National Geographic)

National Geographic's Amazon: Land of the Flooded Forest. (National Geographic)

The Sights and Sounds of South America. (Video Knowledge Learning Library)

Simon Bolivar: The Hispanic and Latin American Heritage Video Collection. (Schlessinger Media)

Web Sites

www.embavenez-us.org

www.internet.ve/wildlife/introd-amazonas1.htm

www.orinoco.org

Due to the dynamic nature of the Internet, some web sites stay current longer than others. To find additional web sites, use a reliable search engine with one or more of the following keywords to help you locate information about Venezuela. Keywords: *Barquisimeto, Caracas, Hugo Chavez, Maracaibo, Orinoco, PDVSA, Simón Bolívar, Waraos.*

Index